"I never promised I could offer you happily ever after."

Knowing that and hearing it were different animals. It felt as if someone were tearing her heart into pieces, bit by agonizing bit.

"I never expected you to," Tory acknowledged. While she appreciated Clayton's directness, she wasn't in any huge hurry to hear him share any more of it. "While I genuinely care about helping you clear your name and, by association, mine, I'd be the first one to stand up and shout that there is no future in this. That being the case, there also won't be any more sex in this."

"Fine by me," he returned easily.

Too easily. But this wasn't the time or place to contemplate the utter foolishness of allowing herself to fall in love with an escaped convict who just happened to be her husband.

Dear Harlequin Intrigue Reader,

This month you'll want to have all six of our books to keep you company as you brave those April showers!

- Debra Webb kicks off THE ENFORCERS, her exciting new trilogy, with *John Doe on Her Doorstep*. And for all of you who have been waiting with bated breath for the newest installment in Kelsey Roberts's THE LANDRY BROTHERS series, we have *Chasing Secrets*.

- Rebecca York, Ann Voss Peterson and Patricia Rosemoor join together in *Desert Sons*. You won't want to miss this unique three-in-one collection!

- Two of your favorite promotions are back. You won't be able to resist Leona Karr's ECLIPSE title, *Shadows on the Lake*. And you'll be on the edge of your seat while reading Jean Barrett's *Paternity Unknown*, the latest installment in TOP SECRET BABIES.

- Meet another of THE PRECINCT's rugged lawmen in Julie Miller's *Police Business*.

Every month you can depend on Harlequin Intrigue to deliver an array of thrilling romantic suspense and mystery. Be sure you read each one!

Sincerely,

Denise O'Sullivan
Senior Editor
Harlequin Intrigue

CHASING SECRETS
KELSEY ROBERTS

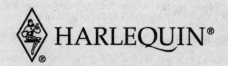

TORONTO • NEW YORK • LONDON
AMSTERDAM • PARIS • SYDNEY • HAMBURG
STOCKHOLM • ATHENS • TOKYO • MILAN • MADRID
PRAGUE • WARSAW • BUDAPEST • AUCKLAND

For Cherry Adair:
Thanks for sharing your incredible time and talent.
You are a great writer but an even more amazing friend.

ISBN 0-373-22839-2

CHASING SECRETS

ABOUT THE AUTHOR

Kelsey Roberts has penned more than twenty novels; won numerous awards and nominations; and landed on bestseller lists, including *USA TODAY* and the Ingrams Top 50 List. She has been featured in the *New York Times* and the *Washington Post,* and makes frequent appearances on both radio and television. She is considered an expert in why women read and write crime fiction, as well as an excellent authority on plotting and structuring the novel.

She resides in south Florida with her family.

Books by Kelsey Roberts

HARLEQUIN INTRIGUE

248—LEGAL TENDER
276—STOLEN MEMORIES
294—THINGS REMEMBERED
326—UNSPOKEN
    CONFESSIONS†
330—UNLAWFULLY WEDDED†
334—UNDYING LAUGHTER†
349—HANDSOME AS SIN†
374—THE BABY EXCHANGE†
395—THE TALL, DARK ALIBI†
412—THE SILENT GROOM†
429—THE WRONG MAN†

455—HER MOTHER'S ARMS†
477—UNFORGETTABLE
    NIGHT†
522—WANTED: COWBOY†
535—HIS ONLY SON*
545—LANDRY'S LAW*
813—BEDSIDE MANNER*
839—CHASING SECRETS*

†The Rose Tattoo
*The Landry Brothers

CAST OF CHARACTERS

Clayton Landry—Convicted of a crime he didn't commit, Clayton finally has a chance to clear his name. But in order to do so, he needs to kidnap the woman who sent him to prison.

Victoria DeSimone—Her testimony helped put Clayton behind bars, but Victoria knows her former boss is innocent. She'll do anything to help set him free…even become his wife.

Pam Landry—The murder of Clayton's ex-wife leads to a trail of lies…and Pam's surprise double life.

Michael Greer—His claim that Clayton had to know something about Pam's hidden fortune sends Clayton and Victoria on a mission to uncover some long-buried secrets.

Seth Landry—As sheriff, Seth had a duty to bring Clayton to justice. But as a brother, he would do anything to see the Landry name cleared.

Chandler Landry—The local news anchor had to report on Clayton's jail break, but that didn't mean he couldn't do some work behind the scenes.

Chapter One

Thunder crashed outside. Inside, the framed photograph of her parents rattled against the mahogany nightstand. A bolt of lightning crackled. The shadows in her bedroom were momentarily dispelled in a flash of bright white.

Victoria DeSimone grumbled and yanked the extra pillow over her face in an attempt to soften the harsh sounds of the storm raging well into its second hour.

The violent weather wasn't all that uncommon for Montana in September. A war was being waged in the black skies above the mountains in the distance. Air, heated that afternoon by an unusually warm sun, was pitted against cooler air rolling down from the north. The battle had produced one of those freakish moments—thunder snow. More accurately, thunder slush. Huge drops of rain pelted against the window and then clanged against the downspout. Intermingled with the rain came periods of heavy, wet snowflakes. She reminded herself that large flakes were good. They meant the snow wouldn't amount to much, if anything.

And that was good. Especially for a nonnative. She kicked at the quilt bunched around her legs. She hated thunder snow. She hated rain. Most of all she hated Montana.

Seven years ago it had seemed like a great idea. Move out into the shadow of the Rockies. Do something dramatic. Commune with nature. Experience the freedom of the great outdoors. She didn't recall reading anything about thunder snow. Or the reality that the fresh, crisp air was freezing.

The great outdoors was great unless you needed a quart of milk. Whoever wrote the chamber of commerce welcome brochure left out the part about distance.

Tory missed Baltimore. She missed walking to grocery stores. She missed feeling as if she was part of a neighborhood. She missed pizza delivery. Hell, she missed pizza, period. Montana had great barbecue sauce, but she hadn't met a single person who could make red sauce.

She was beginning to think that no matter how long she lived in Montana, she would forever be an outsider. Like most Americans of Italian descent, she talked with her hands. In Montana, people worked with their hands. Many only talked when they absolutely had to. You needed pliers to get a simple "hello" out of some people.

She stilled when she heard a noise out in the living room. Soundlessly she listened intently. Nothing but the sound of her own breathing beneath the cushion of the pillow.

"Must have been the storm," she muttered. "Or those friggin' cats!" One of her neighbors ran something akin to a shelter for strays. It didn't seem to matter to the woman that she lived on the second floor. Nope, she just rigged a two-by-four out of her bathroom window allowing the cats to jump from the nearby tree onto the board. Then they could mosey on in whenever the mood hit.

It was a nice sentiment, but the woman apparently didn't realize that not all cats were acrobats. The noise Tory just heard was probably one of the less-gifted animals falling onto the roof of the trash shed. The cats didn't seem to mind. They would land, regroup, then scurry up the tree again, making the leap toward a warm blanket and free food.

Burrowing deeper beneath the pillow when another bolt hit, Tory began making a list of possibilities. She would move someplace warm. Very warm. Amazingly warm. With warm water fit for swimming.

The lakes in her area were fed by mountain streams. You couldn't swim in Montana. You could take a dip. A very quick dip. Natives called the water refreshing. Tory called it intolerable. Water below fifty-five degrees was painful.

Yes, warm water, warm air and air-conditioning. Maybe even steamy, like Louisiana. That would definitely be a change. Good food, parties, crowds. Yes, maybe Louisiana.

It was definitely time to do something. In the four years since the trial, she hadn't exactly adapted. She had promised herself she would give it time—see if it would grow on her. It had. It grew old. She hated shoveling mounds of snow just to find her car. And winters that lasted to Memorial Day and returned in August.

She made the brash, bold decision to move West. She had long since admitted to herself that it had been a bad decision. The problem now was fear of taking another bold, brash step into the unknown.

She shoved the pillow aside at the same instant another flash of lightning filled the room.

"It could be worse," she whispered.

Then she saw the outline of a man.

A man holding a knife.

"Don't scream." His tone was a low command.

"Oh, my God!" Tory yelped, recognizing the voice a split second before another bolt of lightning flashed, illuminating his face.

Her former boss moved closer, until his thighs met the edge of her bed. Tory struggled with the mangled sheets, blankets and pillows tethering her to the bed.

"I mean it, Tory," he repeated softly. "This doesn't have to get ugly."

"Mr. Landry, I'm not a fan of ugly," she assured him, appreciating the gravity of her situation.

He let out a slow, pained breath and reached for her.

Tory swallowed the urge to scream as his hand snaked toward her head and then veered to the lamp. Suddenly the room was bathed in soft, constant light.

Her mouth opened as she looked up at him. Clayton Landry's dark hair clung to his face and neck in dripping strands. She frowned. The filthy orange jumpsuit was drenched and darker in color near a torn slit on the left side.

Oh, my God! He was bleeding!

She rubbed her face, half hoping this was some sort of weird dream brought on by having eaten the entire frozen pound cake she had chiseled out for dinner.

"You're hurt," she stated, watching the red stain darken the jumpsuit that hung limply from his shoulders.

It was hard to fathom that he was the same man she had worked for for three years. His handsome features had hardened, and he seemed to have aged almost a decade in half that time.

He shrugged. "Fairly common hazard in prison."

"What happened?" she asked. "I heard your appeal was denied, so—" She blinked twice, then swallowed. "They don't release you from prison in the jumpsuit, huh?"

"Nope."

"Or with a stab wound?"

"You always were bright."

Folding her hands in her lap, she met his angry gaze. "Did you come here to kill me?"

He laughed, but there was no humor in the sound. "I fantasized about it a time or two while I was earning one dollar and seventeen cents a day taking catalog orders."

Tory shoved some stray strands of hair off her forehead. "Catalog orders?"

He smiled without any real emotion. "Sure. Lucky for me the prison system realizes the benefits of a good education. I got to bypass kitchen and laundry and go right to work in the computer center taking telephone orders from unsuspecting customers."

"For regular people?"

He grunted. "Scary, isn't it. A few dozen of the most popular mail-order companies contract with the prison system to man their telephone banks. I often wondered how women would feel if they knew they were ordering their lacy bras and thongs from convicted rapists."

His dark eyes dropped from her face and she could almost feel his visual perusal.

Shock, pride, fear…any number of things kept her from reacting. But mostly it was the knife clutched in his hand.

He let his gaze wander from her face down her body. "Apparently you don't order from *Intimately Yours*."

Tory's spine stiffened as she shook her head. "Did you come here to mock my flannel sleep sweats?"

This time his smile was more genuine. "Actually, after four years in prison, those flannel things look pretty hot."

Tory started to get up, only to have his hand tighten like a vise around her arm. "Don't move."

"I was going to get a towel for you and a robe for me."

"And a telephone?" he added. "Or maybe you're thinking of running."

"I was thinking of both," she responded with candor. "But we both know that even injured, you'd get to me first, and I really don't want to die. So, we're back to towels and robes."

He kept his hand on her arm but lessened the pressure as he allowed her to stand. He smelled like rain and perspiration. Cold water had pooled by the bed, chilling her bare feet.

"We'll do this together."

Tory felt every inch of his solid body as they moved as a single unit around the bedroom. Prison had hardened more than just his face. His body was like a wall of granite.

"Now we're both wet," Tory stated pointedly as she moved just in front of him to reach the towel rack in the small bath adjoining her bedroom.

"Minor inconvenience," he quipped. He took the towel and stood blocking her in the small bathroom as he began to wipe his face and rub his hair.

Tory blotted the wet patches on her clothing, keeping her eyes in the general direction of the knife still gripped in his hand.

"Mr. Landry, I—"

"Clayton," he corrected as he reached for the top button of the jumpsuit and opened it.

"Mr. Landry, I don't know what has happened, but I'll be more apt to help you if you don't rape me."

His head snapped up and he glared at her for a second. "I'm not going to rape you. God, no wonder it was so easy for you to testify against me."

"I didn't have a choice," she retorted, utterly confused.

"They didn't have a body, Tory. Most of the jurors said your testimony was what convinced them I killed Pam."

"I told them I didn't think you could have done anything like that."

"Right after you admitted to having a crush on me."

Tory felt her cheeks burn from the memory.

"I had to answer the questions honestly."

"Your honesty put me in prison."

"What was I supposed to do? Lie?"

"Based on my life these past few years? Hell, yes! I didn't kill my ex-wife."

"I never said you did," she reiterated quietly. She'd had this argument dozens of times, usually with a member of the large Landry family. "I only repeated what I heard you say that day."

"And don't forget your pining heart," he added with venom. "The jury didn't believe we had never slept together in spite of your claims. You gave them a motive that allowed them to find me guilty."

"That's not my fault. I told the truth and I testified that I never even told you about my…my interest."

"You didn't have to lie, Tory, but you could have been a little more vague. Did you really have to remember every nasty argument my wife and I had in the three years you worked for us?"

"I have a great memory. It's a gift."

He opened the buttons to the waist, then shrugged one arm out of its sleeve.

"Ohmygod," Tory gushed on a breath.

"It's just a scratch," he insisted, though he winced as he bent to get a better view of the injury. "I need some antiseptic and superglue."

"Glue?"

He cast her an annoyed glance. "You want to stitch it closed for me?"

She swallowed the disgust that came from the mere suggestion, and shook her head. "Here's antiseptic," she said, reaching into the medicine cabinet. "The glue's in the kitchen drawer."

"Lead the way," he said, motioning with the tip of the blade.

Tory could feel the warmth of his breath slip beneath the shoulder of her top as he followed her down the narrow hallway. When she reached for the switch, his fingers touched hers. "Don't. Use the light over the stove."

In a very surreal action, Tory pulled out one of the ladder-back chairs for him, and then went to retrieve the glue. She found the tube, then grabbed a handful of paper towels and gave a yank.

Turning, she stopped short and took in the strange sight. Clayton was seated in the chair, stripped to the waist, holding a towel to his injury. His dark hair was mussed, cut shorter than she remembered. His chest, shoulders and arms were sculpted muscle. The remnants of a fading bruise were just a few inches below his collarbone.

The knife was on the table.

Her brain was spinning a kaleidoscope of possibilities. She didn't really have to get hold of the knife. It would suffice to simply shove it away, out of his grasp. Then what? Hope the element of surprise bought her some time? Run like hell?

Clayton's head was still bowed as he said, "Don't try, it won't work. I don't need a knife to hurt you."

That was a chilling reality check. Tory stepped forward and passed him the tube of glue at arm's length.

He regarded her through thick, inky lashes for a second. "I also don't have any desire to hurt you. At least not at this very instant."

"Comforting." She handed off the paper towels.

"Right now I need you."

Years ago she would have swooned at those words. Probably fallen at his feet, torn off her clothes and insisted they have sex then and there.

As if reading her mind, he rolled his eyes. "Not *that* kind of need," he corrected. "Though it has been a while, and after I've swallowed a few aspirins, I might be able to rise to the occasion."

She wasn't sure if she was more mortified that her thoughts were so transparent or that he was so adept at reading them. In any event, it made her feel vulnerable. *Vulnerable* sucked.

"Aspirin thins the blood and you've already spilled enough on my floor. I've got some nonaspirin stuff."

She turned and he sucked in a hard breath.

Spinning on the balls of her feet, Tory turned back to find his face scrunched in agony, the glue stick held inches from the wound. "What?"

"Stings," he said through clenched teeth.

"Baby," she muttered.

"You glue *your* skin together and see if it makes a man out of you," he suggested, wiping small beads of perspiration off his upper lip.

He leaned back in the chair and stretched one long leg out in front of him. His head tilted back and rested against the wall. Exhaustion strained his handsome features, producing deep lines by the corners of his eyes. He took deep, purposeful breaths.

She felt the table edge against her thigh. "Why didn't you go home?"

Her forefinger touched the tabletop.

"The ranch is probably crawling with cops and prison authorities. I didn't want to get my brothers in trouble."

Three more fingers.

"You didn't have that problem with involving me?"

Her pinky touched the hilt.

"One, you owe me. Two, I need information from you. And three—"

His hand was on hers before her brain even registered his movement.

"Three, you don't want to piss me off, do you, Tory?"

"Not really," she admitted, withdrawing her hand to let it fall to her side. "Can't fault a girl for trying."

"Look," he began, then let out a long breath. "I am not going back to prison until I find out who killed Pam."

A pang of sympathy banged against her ribs as she sat down across from him. "I'm sorry about what happened."

"Yeah, I got your letters."

"I wasn't sure. You never responded."

Clayton chuckled. "I didn't really want us to be prison pen pals."

She cringed inwardly, recalling the very letter in which she had made that suggestion. "I only thought you might want some contact with people outside your normal—"

"There's nothing normal about prison."

"Right. I know. I just wanted you to know how badly I felt about your conviction."

Though seated, they were eye level, and Tory found herself looking directly into his eyes. They were the color of imported coffee. He had the Landry genes, selected and perfected over the generations to produce only the finest and fittest of the human species.

Jasper, Montana, had been growing his family for hundreds of years. The current crop included seven sons, Clayton being the middle child. Tory had been in-

timidated by the court proceedings, but that was nothing when compared to the hostile wall of testosterone
created when the brothers stood together. The oldest was
Sam, an investment broker. Seth was the sheriff of Jasper. Chance was a well-liked general practitioner in
town. Chandler was the beloved anchor of WMON-TV.
Cody was a U.S Marshal. Only Shane, the youngest,
worked the vast Lucky 7 ranch.

Individually the Landrys were accomplished, successful men. As a group they were a formidable enemy.
Tory knew that firsthand. The Landrys were rich and in-
fluential, and any person shunned by the Landrys was
shunned by the entire community. Tory had been forced
to go all the way to Helena to find another job after the
trial. No one wanted to hire the woman responsible for
sending a Landry to jail.

"What do you know about the money?"

Tory blinked back to the present. "What money?"

"*The* money. Pam's money."

"Pam didn't have any money," Tory replied. "She
was very clear about that. Why do you think Pam had
money?"

"We'll get to that," he said, hedging. "We're going
to need money. How's your bank account?"

She shrugged. "I've got about fifteen hundred dollars
in my checking account and maybe six or seven thousand dollars in CDs."

"Paralegal salaries have gone up since my incarceration."

"I'm at Dryer and Blane in Helena now," she explained. "They pay very well."

His face registered recognition of the name. It was one of the largest and most prestigious law firms in Helena. He probably didn't know that to get the job she'd had to grovel openly at the interview. Nor did he know that her duties were limited to supporting roles. Even though she was trained in litigation, the firm made sure she was always out of sight of clients and waist-deep in paperwork.

"No other sources of income?"

She shook her head. "Look around, Mr. Landry. Do you see the trappings of a posh lifestyle?"

He did look around. Then said, "Very homey. I never would have pegged you as the crafty type."

"I'm not. I go to craft fairs," she explained. She held up her hands. "Can we back up a bit, please? I don't understand why you're here. Or why you're stabbed. Or pretty much anything."

"I'm here because I broke out of prison tonight."

"How?"

"You know I was moved to Hendersonville?"

"The minimum-security facility? Yes, I read the papers."

"We had an incident there tonight, and an opportunity presented itself."

"What opportunity?"

"One that allowed me to escape."

"Were you stabbed during the escape?"

He shrugged his arm back into the jumpsuit. "Nope. That happened earlier."

"When?"

"When I killed a man."

Chapter Two

Six Hours Earlier

"Line up," the guard's voice boomed out of all six of the speakers mounted along the rectangular room. Two dozen men, clad in orange jumpsuits, shuffled from their workstations.

Clayton was one of those men. The computer terminal he called home for seven and one-third hours every day began to shut down. The machine was controlled by a mainframe in another location.

It was a perfect metaphor for his life—correction, his existence. Every second of his day was controlled by the prison system. He was awakened every day at four forty-five. He had exactly six minutes to dress and brush his teeth, then it was time to stand in line.

Prison, he discovered during his four years in hell, involved a lot of standing in line.

During the three months since his transfer to the minimum security facility, little about his daily routine had changed. Get up, inmate count, breakfast, inmate count, work, inmate count, lunch, inmate count, activity period, inmate count, work, inmate count, dinner, inmate count, free activity, inmate count, lights out, inmate count.

This prison was better than the last in one respect. He was now housed with a better class of prisoner. He smiled at the irony of a Landry having intimate knowledge of the prison caste system. He smiled to himself at the absurdity of it, wondering when he had discovered the prison class system.

The air was thick with the scent of fruity air freshener. He stood perfectly still as the guard began scanning the wristbands that identified each man in line. He could hear voices from the common room just down the hallway. The white-collar criminals enjoyed playing along with the afternoon game shows. From the sound of it, three inmates wanted the contestant to take oceanography for one hundred; two others were in favor of Civil War generals.

Unlike the last facility, Clayton felt fairly certain that the common room wouldn't erupt into violence. Most of the eleven hundred men sharing his address were convicted of nonviolent crimes. Many were white-collar—tax cheats, embezzlers and the like. For most of them, crime had been a matter of opportunity and not a way of life. They were the upper echelon of the prison population.

Next came the transitional guys—men who were near or at the end of their sentences and preparing to be reintroduced to society. They were on their best behavior because the end was in sight. Regardless of the nature of their crimes, these men were focused on one thing—freedom.

Clayton was on the next rung. Not the very bottom, but close to it. He was one of the men who had earned the right to be in the facility regardless of the fact that he had been branded a murderer. Contrary to popular belief murderers were not the most dangerous criminals. In fact, they had the lowest recidivism rate of all felons. That was probably due to the fact that most murders were crimes of passion.

Passion. Clayton could hardly remember the meaning of the word. His years of incarceration had dulled his emotions.

The lowest of the low, in terms of the prison hierarchy, were the transfers. Those inmates were awaiting assignment to a facility or had a court date pending that required they be near Helena. They ran the gamut from petty criminals to horrific, violent drug lords. The problem was, no one tattooed their criminal history on their foreheads, so there was no way to tell how bad a guy was. Hence, the general population shunned them all.

"Open tier three for commissary!" the guard who had been checking IDs called.

There was a loud buzz, then the glass doors slid open. Clayton walked along the yellow stripe painted down the center of the hallway. The spicy scent of pork barbecue wafted down the walkway.

The prison was laid out like a wagon wheel. The center hub was a glass-enclosed elevated platform where no fewer than three guards manned monitors and elaborate electronic panels that controlled virtually every inch of the prison. The commissary was just past the hub.

Clayton had always loved food. Fine dining had been a favorite pastime. Prison food was sustenance at best. Inedible at worst. On the off chance that he ever got out, he vowed never to eat another bean or slab of white bread.

At night he fantasized about fresh vegetables and steamed fish. Anything that wasn't boiled or fried.

Clayton took his place in the chow line. Like a bunch of oversize schoolchildren, the men all took trays and slid them along a line of chrome shelving as food was deposited on recyclable plates.

He was fairly certain that nothing on his plate would have been acceptable Atkins fare. Robotically, he collected utensils from the bin and moved to one of the long tables near the far right side of the room.

Clayton wasn't antisocial; he just learned it was safer and less complicated to keep to himself. The room buzzed with conversation. He heard snippets about one man's family coming for a visit for the upcoming weekend. Another was about a NASCAR event scheduled to be televised. Still another about a trial judge's record on sentencing.

Inmates often sought Clayton out once they heard he'd been an attorney on the outside. After the requisite amount of ribbing, his advice was solicited on everything from the constitutionality of search warrants, to petitioning for Cert from the Supreme Court.

Aside from his duties taking catalog orders over the Internet, Clayton often assisted inmates with their legal troubles. It helped the time pass.

He was chewing the third bite of starchy potato logs when he was joined at his end of the table by a newcomer. Clayton knew he was new to the facility because he had watched him being off-loaded two days earlier. He had arrived by bus as all prisoners do, shackled to a dozen other men.

"You Landry?"

"Mmm-hmm," Clayton responded.

"Michael Greer," he introduced, holding out his hand.

Clayton eyed it for a second before returning the gesture. "Pull up some table," he offered.

Greer swung his leg over the attached bench and slipped in beside Clayton. "Decent food."

"It's okay."

"I need some help," Greer said between shoveling heaps of food into his mouth.

"Don't we all," Clayton replied, shoving the tray of half-eaten food across the table. "What kind of help?"

Greer managed to cram the contents of the tray into his mouth in less than ten bites. He had the table manners of a Hoover vacuum cleaner, but then again, Clayton hadn't seen too many nominees for the Emily Post Cotillion roaming about.

"What kind of help?" Clayton asked again.

Greer shifted so that he now straddled the seat. He leaned closer, keeping his head dipped. "It's complicated."

Clayton almost laughed at the guy's attempt at privacy. Prison was about as private as a petting zoo. "Most things are."

"I need to know where the money is."

Turning his head, Clayton really looked at Greer for the first time since the man had joined him. He looked to be in his midtwenties, with thick brown hair ground into stubble by a fairly recent trip to the prison barber. His eyes were clear blue, intense and devoid of emotion.

"I'm sorry?" Clayton said.

Small beads of perspiration formed on Greer's upper lip as he tipped his head, directing Clayton's gaze down.

Four years ago he would have been shocked to see a homemade knife fashioned out of a toothbrush. Sadly, this wasn't the first time he'd seen someone brandish a cell-made weapon.

"Look, pal," Clayton began.

Greer cupped the knife but shifted closer so that Clayton could feel the tip of the blade between two of his ribs. "I need to know where the money is."

Clayton's eyes danced around the room. He found no allies among the prisoners and no interest among the smattering of guards. "Chill," he told Greer. "You've got ahold of some really bad information. I don't have any money."

Greer's eyes narrowed to dangerous blue slits of barely contained rage. "Your wife had the money. You killed her. You must know where it is."

Pam? "What in the hell are you talking about?"

The knife blade poked through the fabric of his assigned clothing. Clayton felt a prick as the tip pierced his skin.

"I won't cut you if you tell me now," Greer threatened.

"I'd tell you if I knew," Clayton responded, his mind spinning. He was calculating the time and distance needed for him to safely extricate himself from the situation. "Stay cool."

"Frankie Hilton says different."

"Frankie who?" Clayton asked. He wanted the guy

to talk. If he was talking, he wasn't stabbing, and Clayton hoped the guy couldn't do two things at once.

"Don't be dumb, rich boy. Frankie is tired of waiting."

"I don't know Frankie, so I can't possibly know where his money is."

Greer seemed to be growing frustrated. "Did you leave it with the girl from your office?" Greer pressed.

"What girl?"

"The one that screwed you at your trial." Greer seemed to enjoy sharing that piece of annoying history. "If you don't have the money, she's next on the list."

Clayton tried to bridge the gaps separating Tory De-Simone, his late ex-wife and a sum of money worth dying for. Nothing sprang to mind. He began to rise, with Greer matching his every move. Luckily for Clayton, Greer was a few inches shorter.

Clayton's arms were a fraction longer than Greer's, just enough so that Clayton was able to push Greer back with a minimum amount of damage. He felt a warm dampness at his side but remained focused on the knife-wielding man about to rush him.

Greer seemed empowered from the sight of blood. He cackled and crouched. Clayton took up a defensive stance, his eyes fixed on the knife.

Prisoners had perverse radar for violence. Clayton barely had time to plant his feet when a rush of men encircled them. He was only vaguely aware of an alarm being sounded as Greer rushed him.

Using his arm, Clayton deflected the charge, yanked Greer forward and delivered a blow to the smaller man's neck as he shoved him to the floor.

There was a collective grunt from the inmates, then silence.

Clayton felt himself being shoved to the ground by one of the guard's riot sticks. His eyes remained on Greer. He was facedown on the floor, a stream of blood began to stain his jumpsuit where the knife had stabbed him during the fall.

"Jesus, Landry," one of the guards grumbled on an adrenaline-charged breath. "What the hell happened?"

"He came after me," Clayton insisted as he was brought to his feet.

A squadron of guards appeared to shove the prisoners against the far wall. Procedure in a case like this. One guard went to Greer and checked for a pulse. Clayton felt a wave of relief wash over him when the guard indicated that Greer was still alive.

"Let's get you to the infirmary, Landry," the guard said. "Call for an ambulance for Greer. You can give a statement as soon as you're patched up. Can you walk?"

"Of course."

"When are you guys going to learn to just walk away?" the guard chastised as he led Clayton from the dining area.

"He came after me," Clayton insisted.

"Right," the guard said, disgusted. "Keep your mouth shut, Landry."

"I'm telling the truth." Clayton might as well be proclaiming his innocence to a shoe. The guards rarely heard anything but hollow protestations of innocence and claims of elaborate conspiracies. Clayton's claims—though true—got lost in the quagmire of lies.

"The best thing you can do for yourself is keep quiet and get a good lawyer," the guard counseled.

Been there, did that, got the jumpsuit, Clayton thought. Images of another trial, another guilty verdict and a return to the maximum security facility flashed in his brain. The guard led Clayton out of the main building, onto the fenced walkway that separated the main building from the health-care sections.

He felt the first stab of physical pain since the altercation and stopped in midstride.

"Need a gurney?" the guard asked.

"Just give me a second," Clayton answered.

This being a more relaxed environment, prisoners were only handcuffed entering and exiting the main gate or in extraordinary circumstances. The guard allowed him to lean against the twenty-foot fence and suck in deep breaths of cool air.

The guard's microphone crackled to life. "Go ahead. Over."

"Put the bracelets on your guy. Greer didn't make it."

Clayton's heart stopped for a second. No assault charge. It wouldn't be Clayton Landry, wrongly convicted of manslaughter but a model prisoner, versus his attacker. Now it would be Clayton Landry, convicted of killing once, does it again. The chances that he could prevail under these circumstances were somewhere between slim and none. The question would no longer be in which decade he'd be released, but rather if he'd ever be released.

"Sorry," he said to the guard.

"For what?"

"For this."

Clayton punched the guard square in the jaw. The man fell like a stone. Knowing time was important, Clayton jumped and clawed his way up the fence. Tossing his leg over, he jumped and rolled on the ground. Instantly, lights and alarms flooded the grassy area. He ran full-out for the outer fence. Each stride caused his wound to send a sharp signal of pain to his brain.

He was just a few yards from the fence. Silently he prayed for extremes. "Either let me escape or let them kill me trying."

Chapter Three

"So this guy—Greer—just showed up in your prison asking about Pam and money?" Tory asked after she finished dressing. He had been polite enough to allow her to pull on some sweats in the bathroom, providing she left the door open.

Clayton nodded. "Know anything about it?"

She blinked at him. "Of course not. Do you think I would have stayed quiet if I knew something that could have potentially helped you?"

"Yes."

Tory let out a breath of frustration. "I don't know anything. Not about money, not about Greer and not about Frankie Hilton. So, you can leave now."

"Didn't you hear what I said?"

"Every word. I just can't help you with any of this."

Clayton stood. He was quite the intimidating figure standing there, stripped to the waist, expression hard and unyielding. "Greer mentioned you."

"So what?" she countered. "My testimony made the evening news and all the local papers."

"Speaking of the news and local papers, we've got to get out of here."

"We?"

He rolled his eyes. "If you are involved, I want you where I can keep an eye on you. If you aren't involved, then Frankie will send someone after you."

The thought that someone would be after her was simply ludicrous. That happened in horror movies and bad Gothic novels. Not in modern-day Montana. Speaking of which, she added *escaped convict showing up on my doorstep* to her list of reasons to leave Montana.

Tory reached out to the counter and retrieved her purse. Removing her ATM card, she held it out in his general direction. "Feel free to clean me out. I guess that's the least I can do for you."

His dark head tilted slightly as thunder crashed just beyond the window. "Until I get to the bottom of this, you're staying with me."

Tory thought about arguing. She thought about crying. She even considered overpowering the man. None of those options held a scintilla of hope for success. Nope, she needed to focus and use her brain to get out of this.

"Plotting your escape?" Clayton asked.

Tory shrugged. "Do you have a plan?"

"Maybe," Clayton said as he walked to her refrigerator and looked inside. "Don't you shop?"

She tossed her purse back onto the counter after putting her ATM card away. "I don't like cooking for just myself." *Seriously stupid!* she chastised. An armed man has broken into my home and I'm explaining my grocery-buying habits? "I'd be happy to run to the store."

That elicited a small smile from the man. "I'm sure you'd jump at the chance. But you're stuck, Tory."

"Mr. Landry—"

"Clayton for God's sake." He took the half-empty carton of fried rice and placed it in the microwave. He shifted the knife from hand to hand as the need arose. "Are you sure you've never heard of Michael Greer or Frankie Hilton?"

She thought for a minute and then shook her head. "No Michael, no Greer, no Frankie. The only Hilton I know is the hotel I stayed in on a family trip to Florida one year. As I recall, they had nice towels."

He didn't appear to have much use for her humor. At least, not if the scowl was any indication. He went from drawer to drawer until he found the utensils. He placed a large helping in his mouth, then attempted, unsuccessfully, to blow and chew at the same time.

"The microwave is new," she offered, "it makes things really hot."

"Thanks for the warning." He returned to the fridge and got a bottle of water, then took a long drink.

"Sorry for not being up on hostage etiquette."

"Were you always this much of a smart-ass?"

She nodded. "Maybe not. But I'm feeling a little tense right now, so I may not be on my best behavior."

After finishing off the leftover Chinese, he moved on to devour five slices of cheese, two apples and the lone banana. His eating binge gave her some time to think. She honestly didn't believe he'd hurt her, but she had no desire to become entangled in his current legal mess. She needed him out of her house. That was paramount.

"The police are bound to come looking for you here," she said as he polished off the bottle of water.

"Not for me, but I'm sure they're looking for the car I…borrowed. This country tracks stolen cars better than anything else. Do you have any idea how many felons get caught because they're either driving stolen cars or driving poorly? No—" he paused and leveled her with his gaze "—I don't suppose you've had the opportunity to get to know too many felons."

"Not personally, no."

"Well, the cops may not connect you and me anytime soon, but I'm sure they'll have an alert out on the Volvo."

"You stole a Volvo?" she repeated.

"It was handy. After running three miles through the woods in the rain I wasn't being too picky."

"I thought that was a safe car."

"It is unless you leave the keys in the ignition while you're in a convenience store."

"I can't believe you escaped from prison."

"The gods were smiling on me," he offered easily. "If lightning hadn't downed the tree by the gate, I'm sure two dozen vehicles would have been on me like white on rice. I got lucky."

"I don't suppose you'd be willing to consider turning yourself in?"

His reply was nonverbal, but it conveyed his thoughts completely. "I trusted the system once, twice if you count my failed appeal. I won't make that mistake again."

"Where are you going?"

"We?"

"You," she repeated.

He rubbed his face with one hand, absently twirling the knife in the other. "Are you absolutely sure those names mean nothing to you?"

"Positive."

"Pam and money don't ring any bells, either?"

"Not even a faint chime." Tory watched the knife blade reflect a prism of color against the ceiling. "Mrs. Landry didn't exactly treat me like a confidante, and besides, the only time she ever spoke of money was to whine about—"

"Me not giving her enough?" Clayton finished. "Well, unfortunately I didn't understand how important money was to Pam until after we were married."

"The fact that she chased you like a dog and then clung to you like a barnacle wasn't a clue?"

He grinned again. "It was flattering to have the prettiest girl in town interested in me."

"Ego and testosterone are a really bad combination."

"I think I've more than paid for my lapse in judgment, don't you?"

"Maybe."

"I divorced Pam, I didn't kill her."

"I agree," Tory stated easily. "But your little escapade tonight isn't going to work in your favor."

"I know that. But when I heard that Greer had died, I just freaked out a little bit."

Tory's phone rang, and Clayton pounced like a leopard. She was plastered with her back against him, his knife in the general direction of her throat.

"Who is that?" he demanded in a gush of hot air against her ear.

The phone rang a second time.

"I think someone's got the wrong number," she surmised. "I don't usually get calls in the middle of the night. What do you want me to do?"

The phone rang a third time.

"The wrong number?"

"I get a lot of hang ups. Beats the breather who used to call."

The phone rang a fourth time.

"Pick it up. Hold it so I can hear the caller."

She did as instructed. "Hello?"

"Is this Victoria DeSimone?"

"Yes."

"This is Seth Landry." Tory felt every muscle in his body go rigid. The voice on the other end dripped with hostility, and she secretly wondered what bet Seth had lost to be the one forced to contact her. The Landry brothers had made it quite clear that they hated her to the very core.

"Yes, Sheriff?"

"I was calling to ask if you'd heard from my brother."

"Why would I hear from your brother?"

"You're right. Sorry to have bothered you." The line went dead.

"He sounds worried," she offered as she replaced the phone.

Clayton ignored her for the moment. His mind was on hang ups and crank calls. "When did the calls start?"

"What calls?"

He turned her so that she was standing in front of him. His fingers still gripped her upper arm. She smelled of soap and faint jasmine, and his concentration wavered. With her head tilted back, long strands of pale honey-colored hair spilled halfway down her back. It had been short the last time he'd seen her. Trimmed in a functional fashion that he once guessed was a lame attempt to make herself look less appealing.

It was unsuccessful. She had the kind of beauty that other women envied and every man noticed. She floated through life on varying degrees of stunning. Not fashion-model flashy; no, she had a classic, genetically culled beauty. Everything was symmetrical. Her eyes were like starbursts—traces of greens and golds, exploding with energy. Her skin tone hinted at a Mediterranean heritage—smooth, perfect, ageless. Her mouth was an invitation. It took a Herculean effort of will to keep him from dipping his head to brush his lips against hers.

Her tongue slipped out to moisten her lower lip. Clayton swallowed the groan of need clogging his throat. "What calls?"

He set her away from him, more for his comfort than her own. Rape would never enter his thoughts. Seducing her was a whole other thing. A thing he couldn't indulge. Not now at least.

"The hang ups. When did they start?"

Raking her hand through her hair, she answered, "After the breather calls. I'm guessing some kids were getting their jollies trying to scare me."

"What did you do?"

"I breathed back," she admitted with a glint of satisfaction.

"Did they stop?"

"Eventually."

"Did you report the calls?"

She rolled her eyes. "No real harm done," she insisted. "It was usually right after work, usually on Fridays."

"There was a pattern, and you didn't do anything about it?"

"The pattern was most likely some poor thirteen-year-old who liked the sound of my voice, killing time on a Friday night while he waited for his weekend father to pick him up."

"Quite a little scenario you've created there."

"It's the one that made sense," she retorted, annoyed.

Clayton almost laughed aloud. Aside from the first few minutes in the apartment, she was cool and collected. Apparently it didn't faze her to be held hostage, but mock her intellect and she was peeved. "After the heavy breather, you got hang ups?"

She nodded. "Yep. Though only once late at night. Normally he only calls once or twice a week. Around dinnertime."

"You never thought to get caller ID? Or file a police report? They can trace the calls pretty easily. Hell, you can get a service that allows you to trace the calls."

"I know that," she said defensively, crossing her arms in front of her chest. "I got that service and did the star thing, but the number is blocked."

"Did you ever think there was a connection between Pam's death and the phone calls?"

"Four years apart? No."

Point taken. "Did anything happen a year ago?" he pressed.

He noticed a slight hesitation before she shook her head. "No."

"We've got to get out of here. If Seth called you, then I'm thinking the cavalry won't be far behind. You don't happen to have anything I can wear, do you?"

"A thong and a sports bra?"

He did laugh, in spite of himself. "You're quite the wise-ass."

"It happens when I'm nervous," she admitted. "Stress brings it out in me."

"I'm a little obvious in this orange jumpsuit," he thought aloud.

"Two D."

"What?"

"The guy in 2D leaves his clothes in the dryer sometimes. We can check the laundry room."

Tory was permitted to take her purse, her coat— pretty much everything she might take if she was going out. Only, this wasn't a date, this was a kidnapping. Clayton's knife was ever present, but he seemed to keep it by his side instead of poised and ready.

Good. Lull him into a false sense of security and then bolt. That was the plan.

As expected, 2D had a pair of jeans and a Dead Head shirt in the dryer along with a mismatched pair of socks. The jeans were about an inch short and the T-shirt was so snug that Jerry Garcia looked like a furry Asian caricature.

"Maybe the jumpsuit is better," Clayton suggested as he pulled on his waterlogged sneakers.

"I've heard the clothes make the man."

"Ever hear that you shouldn't piss off the guy with the knife?"

She shrugged. "Now what?"

"The ranch."

"Are you nuts?" she yelped. "That place has to be crazy with cops and wardens and—"

"Wardens don't chase escaped prisoners."

"Whatever," she dismissed. "You can't go there, Clayton, they'll arrest you on the spot."

"I can't," he agreed. "But you can."

Chapter Four

Approaching the exit of her building, Tory was keenly aware of Clayton's presence. It would have been hard not to notice, since she was plastered full against him.

Clayton jerked her to a stop, then reached around her to tentatively open the door. The storm had trickled to a misty drizzle, carried on a chilly wind. A cat wailed in the distance. Other than that, there were no signs of life in the small parking lot fronting the building.

She remained resolute in her plan. Get him to wherever, then bolt.

He slipped in front of her, grasping her hand and leading her into the night. Tugging the edges of her jacket together, she wondered if he was cold. Probably not. Not if his adrenaline was pumping the way hers was—pounding in her chest and reverberating in her ears.

"Which one is yours?"

"The black BMW," she returned in a rushed whisper.

He turned and glared accusingly at her in the shadows. "Dryer and Blane apparently pay you quite well."

Pulling the keys from her jacket pocket, she stiffened at his unspoken indictment. "I'm allowed to have a luxury."

"Climb over," he instructed, opening the passenger's door.

With a complete lack of grace, Tory managed to crawl behind the wheel. Clayton slid into the seat next to her. There was something oddly bizarre about the two of them fastening their seat belts before she turned on the ignition.

"Are you going to tell me the plan?" she asked, resting her right hand on the gearshift as the car silently idled in place.

"I'm making it up as I go along," he admitted. "I'm pretty new at being the fleeing felon."

Tory let out a breath and backed out of the parking area. "You're putting yourself in serious danger going to the Lucky 7."

"I'm not going to the ranch."

Quickly she glanced at his shadowed profile. "But I thought—"

"You're going."

"Me?"

"You can get what I can't."

"Which is?"

"Since Pam doesn't have any family, my brothers put the stuff from her office and the house in storage in one of the outbuildings on the ranch."

"So we're not really going to the house?" She felt a wave of relief. The Landrys hated her, and she had no desire for a face-to-face confrontation with them. That had happened after her testimony, and she wasn't in any hurry to repeat the scene.

"You are," he corrected. He let out a slow breath that sounded alarms in her head.

"How's your side?"

"It hurts." He shifted in his seat, feeling a haze of fog threatening to cloud his brain. Rubbing his face, he assumed that the slightly off sensation was a result of the stabbing. Hopefully, it would pass. Reaching onto the console, he took her purse and began to rummage through it. He could hear her breathing and knew without being told that she didn't appreciate his intrusion. Women, he knew, were pretty weird about their purses. He found her wallet, cosmetics, a mirror, a tattered ticket stub from a movie theater, a state-of-the-art PDA and a cell phone. "You've got a lot of crap in here," he opined as he flicked a wayward mint off his knuckle.

"If I go to the ranch house, what makes you think I won't call the cops the minute I step in the door?"

He sighed. That was a distinct possibility. Despite her claims to the contrary, there were some pretty incriminating things glaring up at him. First and foremost was the forty-thousand-dollar car. How the hell could she afford this car? Paralegals—even well-paid ones—didn't make that kind of money.

He flipped open the PDA. It, too, was top-of-the-line. The phone was yet another red flag. He turned it in his hand and then studied the keypad. It wasn't just a phone. It was a camera, as well. The car, the electronic toys—they all fed his distrust.

"This is pretty nifty," he said, pressing a button. The phone flashed and he found himself looking at a digital image of most of his face on the small screen.

"A to-me from-me Christmas present," she said, annoyed. "Could you stop playing with the damned phone?"

He closed the flip top and pushed some hair off his forehead. He hadn't been in a car for years and was amazed at how confining it felt. "You very well might turn me in first chance you get."

"It's the sane thing to do," she assured him. "Running like this is dangerous. You could get killed. Even worse, you could get me killed."

Clayton was torn. He knew she was right. The last thing he wanted was her getting hurt or killed because of him. Unless, of course, she was lying and she did know something about the money. Michael Greer had been willing to kill for it, so he guessed the amount to be substantial. If Tory was involved, she'd probably do almost anything to keep control.

He didn't have a lot of options. He didn't trust Tory, but right now he didn't have choices. "Look, I need to find this Frankie Hilton guy. He's the key."

"The key to what?"

"To finding out who killed Pam and framed me."

"So, have your attorney—"

"I've been playing by the rules since my arrest, and it hasn't worked out too well, in case you didn't notice."

Tory turned west to drive through downtown Jasper. Feeling the space between the seat bottom and the door, Clayton found the adjustment lever and reclined his seat. He didn't want to risk being seen. Too many people in Jasper knew him on sight. Not that anyone was likely to be strolling the streets in the middle of the night.

"I'm sure that once you explain what happened, you'll be cleared of the stabbing in the prison and then you can—"

"It doesn't work that way," he broke in harshly. "Look, I don't trust you, but right now I don't have a choice."

"Why wouldn't you trust me?" she retorted.

He was a little taken aback by the hurt in her tone. "Why should I trust you? You worked side by side with my wife. And apparently you were harboring some massive crush on me the whole time."

"First," she began, indignant. "It wasn't *massive,* you arrogant idiot."

"You never said anything to me. In fact, you went to great pains to keep it a secret."

"Ya think? Mr. Landry, you were my boss. My married boss. Did you expect me to walk in one morning and say 'I've indexed the Riley depositions—oh, and by the way, want to do the nasty before your wife comes back from probate court?'"

"I would have turned you down."

He didn't need to see her face to know his intentionally harsh remark had hit its target. He heard the small intake of breath and almost regretted his words.

"You have no reason not to trust me."

"You and my wife were close."

"I worked for Mrs. Landry. I respected her as my boss just as I respected you as my boss."

"And you don't know anything about Pam and money?"

"Yes," she breathed, exasperated. "I know your wife

liked money. Craved it even. Not to speak ill of the dead, but c'mon, Mr. Landry, she was livid when you filed for divorce. She was fit to be tied when the judge ruled your settlement offer fair and ordered the sale of the law practice."

"It was reasonable," Clayton stated, his three-hundred-thousand lump-sum payment was more than adequate compensation for the two years they had lived as man and wife. Personally, he figured she should have repaid him at least fifty thousand for the hell she put him through during their year of separation. He couldn't figure out why Pam had wanted to remain married. She sure as hell didn't love him. She knew he didn't love her, still, she had fought, pleaded, promised and provoked until the day she died.

"She wasn't chummy with me," Tory supplied. "I did the work she assigned to me and nothing more."

"You never talked? Never had a casual drink or anything?"

She made a grunting sound. "No, and neither did we," she pointed out. "I never crossed the line, Mr. Landry."

That much was true. Clayton had to admit he was as shocked as anyone to hear Tory testify that she found him attractive and had, in fact, told at least one neighbor of her feelings. "Then cut me some slack now," he asked, feeling suddenly tired.

"I think I've been pretty patient so far," she retorted. "Be smart. Let me contact the authorities. I'll stay with you until—"

"I can't," he admitted. "Look, I'll make you a deal."

"I'm listening."

"Help me go through Pam's things, get me to a motel out of town and you're free to leave and do whatever."

"That's aiding and abetting. You're asking me to commit a crime," she reminded him.

"No one will know you've helped me."

"They will the minute I go to the ranch."

"You can trust my brothers."

"No," she countered, "*you* can trust your brothers. They hate me."

"I'll swear you acted under threat of death," he insisted. "My brothers won't get in my way."

She sighed. "So what is it you want me to do?"

THE LUCKY 7 WAS a vast spread to the west of Jasper. At one time, Jasper had been part of the vast Landry holdings. The town was named for Clayton's however-many-greats grandfather, and the Landrys wielded considerable power and prestige in the small Montana community.

Tory was alone in the car, approaching the main house like the proverbial lamb going to slaughter. Conflict gnawed at her gut. Her rational, sensible, upstanding-citizen side begged her to stop and tell any one of the dozen or so officials standing around on the porch that she had left Clayton in the woods near the general store a few miles back.

The kind, compassionate, still-half-infatuated-with-my-former-boss side urged her on.

She had barely placed her car in park when a uniformed man came up to her door. After blinding her with a flashlight and shining it through the interior of her car, he opened her door.

"Can I help you?"

Tory swallowed her fear. Fear that Clayton had left some sort of incriminating evidence in her car. Fear that she would panic and blurt out his location at any moment. Fear that she would fail in her mission to help him.

What the hell was I thinking? she wondered as she offered her brightest smile to the middle-aged officer. "I'm Victoria DeSimone. Sheriff Landry called me earlier tonight."

The officer seemed to consider her comment for a protracted second. In spite of the cold, she could feel guilty perspiration gathering between her shoulder blades.

"Mind opening the trunk?" he asked.

Tory felt a shiver of anxiety. Clayton had originally suggested that he hide in the trunk while she went into the house. Luckily she had won that argument.

She pressed the button, and the trunk popped open. The officer began to inspect the interior just as the front door opened.

Tory knew the man silhouetted in the doorway was Shane, the youngest brother. She also knew he was the most likely to toss her off the property.

"What are you doing here?" he demanded without preamble.

Shane had the most unique take on the Landry good looks. He was taller, leaner and appeared less polished than his older siblings. Maybe it was the long hair pulled thoughtlessly into a ponytail at the nape of his neck. Or maybe it was his light eyes. It didn't matter because at this very second he was marching toward her with fists balled at his sides.

Tory felt very much like a deer in the headlights, seeing and sensing speeding disaster yet helpless to get out of the way.

"I came to see if there was anything I could do," she began in a rush of urgent breath.

"Yeah. There is. You can get the hell out of here," he thundered.

The officer examining her trunk, as well as the few others lingering on the porch, stood at attention.

This is going well. Shane stopped just short of bowling her down onto the gravel driveway.

"Haven't you done enough?" Shane accused, his eyes narrowed with pure anger. "You're half the reason Clayton is out there right now."

Following Clayton's instructions, she burst into tears. Loud, sloppy tears. Three massive sobs into her act, Shane cursed, took her hand and led her roughly up the steps.

"Taylor!" Shane called as soon as they had crossed the threshold. "Get her a glass of water and get her the hell out of here."

The pretty young housekeeper appeared in an instant, enveloping Tory in her arms. "What did you do, Shane?"

Tory was amazed at the housekeeper's harsh tone. It didn't seem like the best time to be challenging the youngest Landry. Tory buried her head against Taylor's shoulder and silently thanked the gods. She was inside. Step one accomplished.

"I yelled," Shane shot back. "Help her get it together so she can leave."

"Stop acting like a maniac," Taylor yelled back. "I'm

sure she was only trying to help." She guided Tory down a long, paneled hallway into a brightly lit kitchen.

After accepting a napkin and blotting her completely dry eyes, Tory glanced around. She could see several people gathered in the next room, and a few others clogged the entranceway.

"Th-thank you," she managed as she was handed a glass full of water. She sipped, then looked up to find Taylor eyeing her with a deep frown furrowing her brow. "Please don't ask me why, but I need the keys to the storage shed."

Taylor placed one hand on her hip, studied Tory for a few seconds, then opened her mouth. "Shane!"

Tory's panic welled up like a geyser. Clayton had been adamant that she not involve his brothers directly. Now what?

Shane reappeared, looking worried, angry and annoyed all at once. "What?"

"She needs—"

"More water," Tory interrupted.

Shane regarded her with suspicion. "What are you trying to pull?"

The tension was palpable. Tory was at a loss for another tack. Forget Clayton's desires to keep his family out of this. Time was wasting. "I'm helping your brother," she began in a determined whisper.

"You've done a great job so far."

She didn't have the time or the inclination for his sarcasm. "I need the keys to the shed where Pam's things are stored."

"Why?"

"You'll just have to trust me," Tory replied.

"That's not going to happen."

"Keep your voice down," she insisted. "Look, Shane, Clayton doesn't want you involved, but I need those keys. If we break into the shed, the police are sure to notice since we're sure they're keeping a pretty close watch on this place."

"I don't know what your game is, lady, but—"

Of all times, her cell phone chirped from inside her purse. At first she ignored it. "Clayton doesn't have time for this. Just give me the keys and—" The cell phone rang again. "Dammit!" she huffed as she pulled it from her purse and flipped it open. A text message flashed a single word: *PHOTO*.

She pressed two buttons and retrieved the image. Carefully she turned the small screen toward Shane. "I need your help."

"Get rid of that," Shane insisted in a conspiratorial tone. "What the hell is going on?"

Tory leaned forward, careful to keep one eye on the doorway. The last thing she needed was to have someone catch her with a picture of a fugitive on her cell phone. "No questions, Shane. Just the key."

"Do it," Taylor urged. "She's helping Clayton, that's all you need to know."

"And you can't say a word," Tory insisted. "Especially not to any of your brothers."

"Tell me what the plan is."

Tory rolled her eyes and felt her jaw clench. "We're kind of winging it right now. He doesn't want you involved. I guess I was supposed to show the picture to your housekeeper and swear her to secrecy. I've already screwed that up, so just give me the key and toss me out on my ear."

She started to rise, and Shane grabbed her arm. "I'm not leaving Clayton's fate in your hands. I remember what happened the last time."

She shrugged free and met his icy stare. "You don't have a choice," she promised him. "Use your brain, Mr. Landry. If I wanted to hurt Clayton, I could have told half a dozen people where he is already."

"She's right," Taylor interjected.

"And you know that how?" Shane demanded, turning his attention to the petite woman. "How can you be sure she's on his side?"

"I'm smarter than you are," Taylor replied. "Women's intuition."

"That's the best you can do?"

"On short notice and very little sleep, yes."

Tory waved her hand. "Hello? Back to the present."

The two of them looked like a couple of guilty teenagers caught talking during final exams. Shane hesitated, then went to a small cabinet near the back door and returned with a small silver key.

Glancing around and satisfied that no one in the house was paying them any special attention, he slipped the key to Tory and grasped her elbow. He led her toward the front entrance and leaned close to her ear to say, "Make this work."

"That's the idea."

"She's leaving," Shane told the officer guarding the door. "And she isn't coming back."

Chapter Five

"We are going to get *so* caught," Tory whispered as she applied more effort to the key. The neglected lock wasn't being all that cooperative.

"Hush and keep working," Clayton directed as he stood over her, eyes scanning the buzz of activity about a thousand yards away. He felt as if every law enforcement official within a three-county area was parked on the front lawn of his family home.

Maybe this idea wasn't his best. Too late, already committed.

"Finally!" he heard Tory exclaim, followed immediately by a metal click and the creak of the door opening.

The storage building smelled of pesticides and damp paper. He carefully closed the door before feeling along the side wall for the switch.

A naked bulb dangled on a cord from the ceiling, washing the room in harsh light and flat shadows. Dusty sheets made ghosts of furniture rammed up against the back wall of the rectangular room.

"What are we looking for?" Tory whispered.

"Files, address books, day planners. Anywhere Pam might have referenced Frankie Hilton."

He went to work on the neatly packed boxes to the left while she went to the right. Clayton was relieved and concerned all at once. Relieved that she had done as asked and gotten the key from Taylor, concerned that she might be setting him up.

He half expected a SWAT team to burst through the door. Tory could have easily explained their plans and arranged for the authorities to apprehend him in this isolated place.

"I've got two boxes of brochures and files from various nursing homes Pam must have worked with."

"Anything jump out at you?" he called over his shoulder. He was wrist-deep in Pam's college mementos.

"Not really. I recognize a lot of this stuff. Pam's reports to the state auditors when the estate's assets were sold off. Attached appraisals, pretty standard."

"I know she kept a calendar," he replied, placing the lid back on the box and moving on to another. "We'll put that stuff in the trunk but keep looking for personal stuff."

He heard Tory rustling through papers, and occasionally she would call out the contents of whatever she had uncovered. He was tired, warm and discouraged when he opened the next to last box. There, nestled on top of some more files, he saw the messy, alphabetized disk. "Got the Rolodex!" he called.

"Great," Tory replied. "Do I keep looking?"

"No," he shoved the box toward the door along with three others they had decided to take with them. "We've been here a while. I don't want to overstay my welcome."

He flicked the switch, darkening the storage shed. Carefully Clayton tugged on the door so that he could peer through the small crack. He heard only the gentle movements of the tree branches swaying in the breeze. The cool air felt good. He was really hot, and the fog in his brain seemed to thicken.

"I'll back the car toward the door," Tory offered.

He thought for an instant that this might be the signal. Braced in the doorway, he wouldn't have been totally surprised if floodlights blinded him and a helicopter appeared off in the clearing. He had no guarantees with Tory.

Without using the headlamps, Tory managed to position the car at right angles to the building. The sight of so many law enforcement officers just across the pasture quickened her pulse. *What am I doing?* If one—just one—of the officers bothered to look in their direction, they were toast. And she doubted, very seriously, that they would believe she'd done all this under threat of death.

Clayton moved sluggishly, so she increased her efforts. Carrying one box and shoving a second along with her foot, she managed to get the boxes loaded into the trunk. Clayton was holding the Rolodex as they got into the car and crept back down the service road. Tory was sure each piece of spewn gravel would alert the police. It felt as if it took a few years to reach the main road.

"Where to?"

"Head east," he said, a slowness in his speech that gave her pause.

"Are you okay?"

"I'm not sure," he admitted.

Tory reached out and touched his forehead. "You're burning up."

"I doubt Greer's homemade knife was rinsed and sanitized."

Her already-taxed blood pressure went up another few points. "You need to see a doctor."

"No way," Clayton argued. "Head back to Helena."

"Forget it," she retorted firmly. "You need medical attention."

"Drive the damned car, Tory. I'll take some aspirin when we find a motel."

"You're being stupid."

"I'd rather be stupid than back in jail."

Tory clamped her mouth shut. There wasn't anything she could say that would change his mind, so she'd have to change her tack. First and foremost, she needed to get him someplace warm and comfortable.

Forty odd minutes later she pulled into the parking lot of a convenience store. "Wait here."

The sun was just spilling over the mountains when she slipped her ATM card into the slot. Punching in the codes, she waited for the machine to spit out her maximum daily withdrawal.

She went inside and bought some herbal tea and some energy bars. Returning to the car, she found Clayton looking rather pale but alert. "There's a motel up the road. I'll register there and you can get some rest."

He reached over and took her wrist. Not grabbed. Not yanked—he simply placed his warm fingers against her skin and held her eyes. "Then you leave."

"Something like that," she attempted to deflect the gratitude she read in his expression.

"Really, Tory. You've done enough. With the stuff we got from storage, I'll be able to handle it from here."

"You'll be fine," she agreed, driving out of the lot. "A man with a stab wound, a fever, no money, no car and most of the state of Montana looking for him should have no problem going it alone."

"I mean it," he insisted.

"We'll see."

Good to her word, Tory registered them for two weeks at the Queen of the Rockies Motel a few minutes later. Regardless of how long they actually occupied the room, she figured a long-term rental would raise fewer flags than a one-night stay. It was a single-story establishment with very few cars in the lot. The room was tidy but devoid of frills. It had a bed, a modest bath and a scratched round table with two mismatched chairs. The scent of disinfectant clung to the rust-colored drapes she yanked closed against the bright golden rays of sunlight streaming in the smudged window.

"It's clean," she commented.

Clayton sat on the end of the bed. He offered a weak but compelling smile that inspired a small flutter in the pit of her stomach. "It's a palace," he countered. "A step down for you but a major improvement for me."

"I'll get the first box," she said, insisting he stay in the room. "You're the one wanted by the law."

She could tell it rankled his chivalrous side to allow

her to do all the heavy lifting but it couldn't be helped. Tory stopped only long enough to run a pot of water through the antiquated coffeemaker on the table.

On her second trip into the room, she brought the bag from the convenience store. "Some tea and something to eat might help."

"Finding Frankie Hilton will help," he countered, and began flipping through the Rolodex.

Hot water sputtered into the pot, so Tory poured some into one slightly chipped mug and dropped in the tea bag. If he wouldn't go to the hospital, maybe she could convince him to accept a house call.

"Let me call your brother Chance."

"No way," Clayton adamantly shook his head. "I already told you I didn't want my brothers involved."

"Shane knows," she shot back, utterly frustrated.

His dark head whipped up and he looked positively furious. "How did that happen?"

"It was your fault," Tory responded, meeting his hostile glare with one of her own. "You called the cell phone in the middle of my conversation. I showed Shane the picture."

"You were supposed to show it to Taylor, not my brother."

"It's okay to involve Taylor and me, but Landry men get a pass?"

His eyes narrowed dangerously. "Greer involved you, not me. I was willing to take a chance on Taylor because I figured the cops wouldn't press her and even if they did, Taylor is tough."

"Your brother doesn't come off as a pushover."

"Shane has a temper," Clayton said. "It makes him unpredictable."

"Well, Chance is a doctor."

"And the cops are probably watching him. They know I got stabbed. They're probably expecting me to show up there."

That was true enough. Tory tugged her hair into a ponytail and then twisted it into a lose bun. "Okay," she began, thinking aloud. "You can't contact Chance, but I can."

"That won't be obvious," Clayton grumbled.

"Drink some tea and shut up," she snapped.

"Tea?"

Annoyed, she flexed her fingers and fought off the urge to slap him silly. "It's herbal. It's hot. It's good for you. Stop whining and drink it so I can think."

"It's red. Tea isn't supposed to be red."

"It's cranberry."

"Tea should be brown."

"Shush!" she insisted, placing her finger to her lips.

He muttered something unintelligible. Tory paced across the worn orange carpet. "I can take some pictures of your wound. Write down your symptoms and take all that to Chance. He can decide what you need and—"

"I said no."

Standing a few feet in front of him, Tory planted her hands on her hips and let her gaze drill into him. "This isn't a debate, Clayton. Your choices are to let me go see Chance or I walk out that door and call the authorities and let some prison doctor tend to you. Which is it?"

"Neither, I—"

She took her cell phone from her bag. "Don't think I won't."

Clayton didn't call her bluff. Good thing, too, she thought. She wasn't sure if she could follow through with it.

"There aren't any Hiltons in the Rolodex." Clayton informed her, clearly disappointed. "At least not under *H* or even *F.*"

After unwrapping an energy bar for him, Tory went about writing down his symptoms and a detailed description of his wound and storing the data in her PDA. Taking photographs and beaming them to her PDA file, as well, she finished by replacing the bandage.

"Keep the cell phone," she suggested. "I'll call that number if I need any additional information."

"Be careful," Clayton said.

"Take a hot shower and try to get some rest," she suggested.

"As soon as I go through every name and phone number I can find. Tory?"

"Yes?"

"Be careful."

"You, too."

BY MIDMORNING she was in Chance's office.

"He needs sutures," Chance Landry, M.D., announced upon reviewing the digital file she had provided.

"Not a possibility," Tory insisted.

Chance's very pregnant wife was at his side, her expression painted with concern. Valerie Landry worked for her husband and seemed to be the more emotional of the two.

"You have to go to him, Chance," Val insisted. "He needs help."

"That won't work, either," Tory insisted. "Aside from the fact that Clayton doesn't want his family involved, I'm sure the police are watching you, and we can't risk that."

"We?" Val queried.

Tory shrugged. "H-he can't go to Clayton."

Val started to tear up. "Sorry. Hormones. I cry at the drop of a hat these days."

"And if she doesn't like the hat. Or if the hat is the wrong color. Or if—"

Val jabbed her husband lovingly in the ribs. "You strap twenty-five extra pounds around your waist for months and see how chipper you feel."

"I am humbled in your presence," Chance teased. "May I focus on my brother now, or will you see that as yet another lapse of attention on my part?"

Val turned to Tory. "I am not that bad. He's making me sound horrible."

Tory felt a pang of envy. This was a happily married couple. You could see it in the way they constantly touched each other. In the private looks that passed between them. They had magic.

"I can give you some antibiotics, but I want you to go to the pharmacy and get this brand of bandage from Guy. Clayton's got to take the meds and make sure he keeps the wound clean and covered. And tell my brother to stay away from glue."

"I will. Thanks."

Chance took her hand in his. "No, thank you. I don't know why you're doing this, but don't make me sorry I trusted you."

"Ignore him. Landrys look out for their own and sometimes they take it too far," Val opined. "I'll get the antibiotic, and I'll even toss in some olive leaf extract."

"For?"

"Hedging our bets," Val answered.

"A harmless supplement," Chance whispered as soon as his wife was out of earshot. "Who knows, it might help. Val has all sorts of very effective alternative remedies."

"I'll do my best," Tory promised.

Exiting the office, she made her way across the street to a discount store. Luckily she was the only customer, so she promptly rounded up a few supplies and gave the clerk her credit card.

Maybe it was the seesaw of adrenaline over the past twelve hours or maybe it was just her rational mind clamoring to get out. It didn't matter, the result was the same. Tory was wondering yet again what she was doing.

Aiding and abetting.

What if there was no Frankie Hilton? What if Greer had just been some convict with a bad attitude? Clayton would go back to prison, and she would face some jail time, as well.

And just last night she thought the cat woman upstairs was the worst of her problems.

"You wanted a change," she grumbled as she walked back in the direction of her car. "This is definitely a change."

She was a block shy of where the richly colored autumn leaves blanketed Jasper Park. The name on the building called to her as she passed. "Library," she whispered to the wind.

Caught in the moment, Tory took the marble steps two at a time and burst though the doors into the solemn room. Jasper was a small county, but thanks to donations from the Landry Family, the library wanted for nothing.

The computers were located through the reference doors. Tory dropped her purse and the pharmacy bag, but didn't think of removing her jacket as she hastily typed in the password to access her Internet server.

She typed in Frankie Hilton's name but got nothing for her efforts. A second search was more successful. According to the police blotter for the period two weeks earlier, Michael Greer had been convicted of passing bad checks. His guilty plea had impressed the judge and resulted in a sentence of eighteen months at a minimum-security facility. Navigating a few command bars, Tory printed out the information and shoved it into her purse.

She made one more stop before heading back to the motel. Carrying the two largest bags, she slipped the key in the door, only to have it burst open on her.

Instead of falling on her face, she lunged forward and fell onto the bed, bags ripping open.

"You've been gone for hours!" Clayton growled.

Lifting her face off the bed, she rolled over and found her footing. He seemed a bit better, and she guessed at the cause. The tea had been consumed and, judging from the steamy window and mirror, he'd availed himself of the shower.

"I brought you some medicine, some clothes and some information. And not that you asked, but I'm fine."

"Good. Any reason you didn't call?"

Tory opened her mouth but no sound came out. Probably because he was standing in front of her looking every inch like her most secret fantasy. He was stripped to the waist. Dark hair covered his broad chest, then tapered down like an arrow before disappearing into the waist of his jeans. Well, not actually the waist. Nope. The top button was undone. So were her nerves.

Trying desperately not to let her mind wander into dangerous territory, she commanded her eyes to remain fixed on his face. That didn't help much. Not when he had towel-mused hair. Just-got-out-of-bed hair. Nope. Not working.

"The meds are in the car."

Clayton stood between her and the door. His expression was dark and unreadable. "I found Frankie Hilton."

She smiled. "That's great."

"Listen to this," he said, taking her cell phone, hitting the redial button and holding it to her ear.

A few seconds and four rings later, a male voice came on the line, "This is Frankie. Leave a message."

Clayton ended the connection before she could speak.

"That's great," she repeated. "So he was in Pam's Rolodex?"

Chance nodded. "Filed under *D*."

"*D?*" she repeated, confused.

"The name and address were local but I noticed that the area code was Las Vegas so I took a chance."

"Very resourceful," Tory commended. "Lucky for you it wasn't misfiled in the Zs."

Clayton wasn't smiling. "It wasn't misfiled. The local name and address were yours."

Chapter Six

She was either a very good actress or an exceptional liar or both. The end result was Clayton couldn't tell if her shock was genuine or forced.

"What are you implying?" she demanded after her initial surprise waned.

"Nothing to imply. Just fact. Pam listed Frankie's phone number with your name and address. Want to explain that?"

"I can't," she replied honestly. "May I see the card?"

Pointing to the table, he directed her to the card he had been staring at for what felt like hours.

Reluctantly he had to admit he respected the very regal way she strode to the table. It was a struggle to maintain his anger. Then again, years of incarceration had schooled him well in the art of holding his temper.

His brain was foggy, and he felt alternating waves of heat and chills assaulting his body.

"I have no idea why Mrs. Landry would have filed Frankie Hilton's contact information under my name. Unless—"

"This ought to be good," he commented, his words cloaked in undiluted sarcasm.

She glanced up and offered him a penetrating glare. He had to give her credit. She hadn't so much as twitched a guilty muscle thus far. His head pounded.

"Assuming she needed to keep the number handy, this is a perfect place. Hidden in plain sight. A card with Frankie Hilton's name might have been discovered by anyone thumbing through her private directory. How many times did you pass right over my name and address as you were scrutinizing the names?"

"Three times," he admitted. Her logic was impressive, but the speed with which she had summoned an explanation was troublesome.

He rubbed his hands over his face and silently cursed the world. Tory was either a brilliant asset to his quest for freedom or a deadly, calculating conspirator.

"See? Mrs. Landry was a very smart woman."

As are you, he thought. Tory was seated on the edge of the bed, shoulders squared and a decidedly challenging tilt to her chin. Any woman—hell most women—would have shown some sort of fear. Not Tory.

Nope.

She exuded strength. He admired that. He didn't trust her, but the woman was impressive.

Through the haze of his fever-addled brain, he secretly admitted that her inner strength wasn't her only asset. He didn't have to trust her to lust after her. She was an amazingly beautiful woman. Even sleep deprived, she looked like a fantasy.

Clayton stepped back and leaned against the cool

wall. He felt as if he'd been trapped inside a Tim Burton film. Everything and nothing made sense. In just under twenty-four hours he'd managed to attempt to fend off a knife attack, been stabbed, mounted a one-man prison break, kidnapped a woman who might very well be involved in the conspiracy that landed him in jail, and gathered evidence from the ranch.

"So now what?" she asked.

"I'm thinking."

She rose and reached him in three strides. Gripping his elbow, she led him to the bed and gave a gentle tug until he begrudgingly sat. "Stay here while I get the medications out of the car."

He felt as if a house was sitting on his shoulders, so he didn't bother to argue. His life was a perplexing mess.

Tory returned with a small sack from the pharmacy. After explaining Chance's instructions, she tore into the bandages and salve.

He leaned back, putting his weight on one arm to allow her access to his injury. Being a rather petite woman, Tory had to press against his thigh in order to tend to him.

She smelled clean, fresh and slightly floral, and Clayton relished each deep breath. He felt as if a lifetime had passed since his last encounter with a woman. And she wasn't just any woman.

Every detail of the woman before him seemed to penetrate easily the dull fog of his brain. He noticed everything, beginning with the tendrils of blond hair spilling over her shoulder as she worked. He longed to reach out and touch the silky strands, bring them to his face and drink in her scent. He nearly groaned at the thought.

The pale jade sweatsuit did little to hide her assets. He needed only to close his eyes and he could summon the memory of her amazingly perfect body. She had a long, graceful neck that fairly begged to be kissed. Save for the tiny mole near her right eye, her face was positively flawless. Come to think of it, the mole wasn't a flaw but rather an enhancement. It served to draw attention to the amazing kaleidoscope of color rimmed in thick, feathery lashes. Her eyes managed to be green, gold and brown all at once. Her nose was perfectly proportioned. Not that he gave her nose all that much notice. Not when it was in such wondrous proximity to her lips.

There was no doubt in his mind that he could find amazing pleasure with those lips.

His body reacted in a predictable fashion at the mere acknowledgment of her mouth.

Having her this close was a felony waiting to happen. Clayton knew he needed to rein in his baser instincts. Stay focused. Still, the thought of a few hours with her doing what nature intended men and women to do held an amazing appeal. All he had to do was reach for her.

He could snake his hand around her waist and pull her against him. Then he would know exactly how it felt to really hold her. Not like when they'd been at her apartment and trapped in the urgency of escape. No. Next time he would relish the feel of her soft curves. Assuming there would be a next time.

Her knuckles drew softly across his chest as she applied ointment with a soft cotton swab. He sucked in a breath as the painful sting registered in his brain.

"Sorry," she mumbled as she continued working. "Maybe you should shave your chest before I—"

"I've endured a whole host of things during the course of my incarceration, but I'm definitely drawing the line at shaving chest hair."

"It's going to hurt."

"I'll live." Assuming he didn't die from the desire inspired by the feeling of her fingers working on his skin.

"Finished," she announced, examining her handiwork with pride.

Clayton looked flushed, so her concern about infection multiplied. She went back to the bag and got the antibiotic, handed Clayton two of the pills and then grabbed a glass of water from the bathroom. "Take these and then try to get some rest."

Clayton was examining the items she had purchased on her way back to the motel. His deep frown was annoying. "So they aren't the latest fashions from *GQ*," she huffed as he scowled at the khaki pants and oxford-cloth shirt. "My options were limited. At least they're better than the ones you stole from the dryer."

He lifted his head along with one hand. Between his thumb and forefinger, he waved the receipt like a flag. His eyes glistened darkly. "What were you thinking?"

"That you might appreciate having something to wear that wasn't too small?"

"Your credit card?" he prompted.

She nodded. "I wanted to keep my ready cash available. Unless I go to my bank, I have a two-hundred-dollar-per-day maximum withdrawal from the machine."

His shoulders seemed to slump. "What else have you charged?"

"This room and—" her voice trailed off as realization dawned. "I'm leaving a paper trail. Dammit!"

He let out a breath. "It will probably take a day or two before the authorities pull your financials. They'll see the charges and realize Chance helped you."

"Not necessarily," she insisted. "He gave me the antibiotics from his office. There is no way they can connect my purchases back to him."

"That's something," Clayton sighed. "I've got to get out of here."

"You need to sleep," she countered. "You won't be able to help yourself if you're delirious with fever."

"I could sleep if I didn't think the cops would come busting in here at any second," he snapped.

She bristled. "You're the one who kidnapped me at knifepoint. I didn't ask for this, but I've been really damned accommodating. Using my credit card was a mistake, granted, but I would appreciate it if you would not yell at me."

"I wouldn't be in this mess if you hadn't testified against me."

Tory rolled her eyes, then turned them on him like lasers. "Don't blame me. I was subpoenaed. And I didn't testify to anything that wasn't completely true! You did tell Pam you would see her dead that day."

"It was an expression!"

"I know that. But the jury heard that and, coupled with the neighbors hearing the screams, the blood—"

"The blood evidence was garbage," Clayton argued.

"There wasn't much, and the sample was so mishandled that only type could be discerned. My experts couldn't even test it."

"So be pissed at the judge for letting the evidence in. Be pissed at the jury for not scrutinizing the evidence more carefully. But get off my back, because I'm only trying to help you."

"Why is that?" he asked, only slightly placated.

Her fists balled at her sides as she tried to find the answer to his question. She rationalized that sleep deprivation and her recent penchant for criminal subterfuge had turned her normally sharp brain into a massive gray blob.

He moved toward her. "Why help me, Tory?"

Shaking off her fluster, Tory met his gaze. "Maybe because I couldn't help you four years ago. Maybe because you've got a knife. I…I don't know. Does it matter?"

"Not really, I suppose," he admitted quickly. "It does matter that Pam linked you and Frankie Hilton. It matters that Michael Greer died linking you and Pam's money."

Anger, frustration and exhaustion churned in her stomach. Measuring her tone, she began to speak in clipped syllables. "I have no control over what Pam or Greer did. And in case you forgot, I also had no control over you breaking into my apartment in the middle of the night." She was on the verge of tears, a common and almost uncontrollable reaction to being irritated and sleep deprived.

"Well," she said, grabbing blindly for her purse, hoping to get away before the tears in her eyes spilled onto her cheeks. Grabbing her wallet, she yanked the bills free, almost tearing them in the process, and scattered them on the bed. "I'm done helping you. I'm past done. You're an ungrateful creep, and I've got half a mind to call the cops and tell them exactly where to find your sorry rear end."

"What am I supposed to think?" he countered.

His tone was reasonable—almost conversational, and it grated on her very last nerve. "I don't really give a flaming fig what you think."

"Flaming fig?" he repeated with a chuckle.

She glared at him. "I was raised better than to use the actual expression, but don't push me. And *don't* laugh at me. Good luck."

"Where do you think you're going?"

"Home," she said, wiping the tears from her eyes before they fell free.

He moved and stepped in front of the door, blocking her exit. Briefly she considered shoving him aside but figured that was nothing but wishful thinking.

"I'm not laughing," he insisted. "But I need you to do one more thing for me."

"I'm *so* not in the mood to be helpful."

"Last thing. I promise."

Tory made a production out of repositioning her purse on her shoulder. "What?"

"I need a few hours of sleep."

"And I'm fresh as a daisy," she fairly sneered.

"Two hours of sleep," he claimed. "Keep an eye out for cops and let me close my eyes long enough for the medicine to kick in."

"Then what?"

"Then I'm going to find Frankie and get my life back."

"You don't trust me," she reminded him.

Quietly he studied her face. Tory felt the examination more intimately than if he had actually touched her. She was too flustered to think normally and as much as she hated to admit it—even to herself—those pleading eyes and that lopsided half smile pummeled her common sense.

"I have good reason not to trust anyone," he said. "Someone went to very elaborate measures to frame me for Pam's murder."

"It wasn't me," she insisted.

"Maybe. But look at it from my vantage point. I probably wouldn't have been convicted had you not testified to my argument with Pam. Then I get jumped in the cafeteria by a guy I don't know, who mentions your name. The only person who may be able to untangle this mess is listed in Pam's files under your name. You're the only common denominator around."

Listening to him made it sound like some well-orchestrated conspiracy with her at the center. "I agree that it sounds bad, but I really don't know Frankie Hilton and I didn't know Michael Greer, and your wife didn't confide in me. I can't help you."

"Yes, you can," he countered. "You can let me get some sleep, and then I'll take it from there."

Every fiber in her being was screaming for her to leave. It was the smart move, the safe decision. She needed to forget that he'd been imprisoned for the past four years. That he'd been subjected to a horrible existence for a crime she was certain he didn't commit. And she would. As soon as he was rested enough to leave town.

Thirty minutes later she sat stiffly in a chair while Clayton stretched out on the bed. She assumed he had dosed off. Mainly because he hadn't moved.

She was alone with her addled brain and Pam's belongings. Quietly she began to sift through the boxes. Pam Landry had been an organized woman, though Tory didn't need the contents of the boxes to tell her that. In the years she had worked at Landry and Landry, she had seen Pam's skills firsthand.

Unlike Clayton, Pam had limited her law practice to a single area—estates and trusts. She'd maneuvered through the labyrinth of paperwork necessary to catalog, sell and distribute assets. It was a great deal of accounting, and Tory found the work monotonous. Pam had seemed to enjoy the field, especially once she'd developed a reputation and her caseload multiplied. At the time of her death, Pam was handling a few dozen estates. Tory was familiar with the simple ones—those with wills or trust documents and heirs. They were easy, and Pam had been quick to delegate work on those files to Tory.

The more complicated estates—those where the deceased didn't have a will or heirs—were handled exclusively by Pam. She handled all the details: from hunting down heirs, gathering the assets, having them appraised, selling the property and then distributing the proceeds among distant relatives who often didn't even know the decedent existed. Boring with a capital *B*.

Following Clayton's lead, she started looking for

anything out of the ordinary. She found nothing in Pam's work files. Nothing that she didn't expect to find. Until she opened the last box.

Tucked in a file folder, she came across a dozen credit cards with the security stickers still affixed. It struck her as odd that Pam Landry, a woman who loved money, had credit cards she hadn't bothered to activate. Tory laid the cards out in front of her on the table as a plan began to form in her mind.

Before she thought about too much, she grabbed her cell phone and dialed the toll-free number on the back of the first card. She was delivered into the unending hell of an automated phone system.

Undeterred, she followed the instructions and activated the account. She repeated the steps on the first five cards before she hit a snag. The sixth card was active. Or more accurately, she guessed, the account had never been closed. It actually made sense that some of the cards would be updated cards for existing accounts. That was more in keeping with the Pam Landry she remembered. The woman had never met a credit line she couldn't max out.

Taking a piece of water-marked stationery from the end table, Tory returned to her seat to write Clayton a note. She explained that he could use the five credit cards she placed neatly in a stack. She bundled others with a rubber band from her purse and noted that she hadn't called about those accounts. She left the one card that was active separate and suggested that he not use that account since it might have a password or PIN number assigned by Pam before her death.

Tory stole one last, long glance at Clayton. His shirt lay open, exposing her to a very impressive view of his expansive chest. His face was tranquil, his features serene. It reminded her of years ago, when he was almost always the picture of relaxed confidence. The polished man she had known was gone. She only hoped that if and when he sorted out the mystery of Pam's death, he could regain that easy smile and carefree humor.

Ignoring the strong urge to brush a kiss across his forehead, Tory went to the door. Soundlessly she slipped from the room.

As she drove home, she silently hoped that he got caught. At least then she would know he'd be safe from harm. Anything could happen to him out on the run. None of it good.

Twilight painted the mountains a palette of orange, red and gold as she pulled her BMW into the parking spot in front of her building. It seemed like a lifetime ago that she had stolen out into the night with Clayton.

Climbing up to the third floor, she moved down the shadowy hallway and automatically had her key at the ready. She was about to insert the key when she noticed the lock dangling askew from the door. She frowned, wondering how much it would cost her to repair Clayton's illegal entry into her home.

Between the broken lock and the cash she'd left back at the motel, her budget was pretty much shot to hell. She walked inside and shifted her purse on her shoulder. Clayton was right, the thing weighed a ton. Time for the semiannual cleansing of the handbag.

She was tired and hungry and nervous and worried

and every other emotion she could conjure in her mind. She needed a long bath and an even longer night's sleep. Tory didn't bother with the lights but she did shove a small ottoman in front of the door.

Her neighborhood was perfectly safe. Clayton was the first and only break-in she could recall, so she made a mental note to call a locksmith first thing in the morning. As she walked into the bedroom, she was only vaguely aware of the fact that the message light was blinking on her answering machine. She was pretty sure it was Carol, her supervisor. On her trip to Chance's office, she had called in sick—a spur-of-the-moment decision that was probably going to come back to haunt her.

Carol—or somebody—from work probably called, so she'd need to think of an excuse for not answering the phone by the time she returned to work on Monday. She had two days to come up with something.

Tory walked directly into her bathroom. Surely she was a certifiable mess.

One quick look into the mirror and she screamed.

The shrill sound echoed in the small room as she drew back from the figure lurching out at her from his hiding place behind the door.

She felt hard fingers clamp around her throat as she peered up into eyes distorted beneath a nylon stocking.

"Where is the money, Tory? Did you give it to him?"

She didn't answer. Instead, she tried the knee-to-the-groin maneuver to no avail. Her attacker easily sidestepped her attack, shoving her against the hard edge of the vanity in the process.

Small bursts of light blurred her vision as he squeezed

her throat. Blindly Tory groped around the sink looking
for something—anything—to use in her own defense.
Her fingers brushed against the long, triggerlike handle
of the butane stick she kept to light candles.

Her chest hurt from limited oxygen as she fumbled
with the lighter.

Placing it against his cheek, she pressed the ignition
and then smelled the acrid scent of the fibers melting.

She heard a yelp, felt his hold on her slip and took
advantage of the situation. Mustering all her strength,
she shoved him backward, knocking him into the bath-
tub before scrambling out of the room.

Somehow she managed to grab her purse and kick
the ottoman out of the way without losing valuable time.
Her heart was pounding in her ears, so she couldn't tell
if he had followed. She tried to look over her shoulder
as she raced from the apartment, down the stairs. She
was vaguely aware of a door opening but she didn't
know whether it was one of her neighbors alerted by her
scream or her attacker. She didn't care. She was singu-
larly focused on running.

It was dark as she ran from the building, frantically
clicking the unlock button on her key. The BMW
chirped and the yellow lights flashed like a welcoming
beacon.

Tory jumped into the car, rammed the key into the
ignition and tore out of the parking lot in a rush of
squealing tires and burning rubber. Her hands were
shaking. Hell, her whole body was shaking.

"Tory?" she mumbled. *He knew my name!* "Not Victoria." People she didn't know called her Victoria. Or

sometimes Vicky—a nickname her mother had adamantly opposed. "Only people who know me call me Tory."

Like I know so many criminals!

"Think!" she chided as she took in deep breaths of cool air in an attempt to get her body out of panic mode. It didn't help much. Her eyes darted from the road to the rearview mirror like a Ping-Pong ball in rapid play. She even turned her head to check the back seat, almost expecting someone to jump out at her.

She was several miles from home before she realized she was headed for the motel where she had stashed Clayton. It was several more miles before she was able to stop the sobs wrenching from her body.

Fighting the strong desire to run screaming from the car, she parked three units away from the one she'd rented. It took a few seconds of nerve gathering for her to step out from the safety of her locked car. She felt vulnerable and exposed as she tried to walk nonchalantly to the door.

She reached the room and turned the knob after one last glance around to make certain she hadn't been followed. The door opened without a sound and she stepped into the darkened room. Her brain ran several scenarios simultaneously. Some bad, some good: Clayton's infection had worsened and he was unconscious on the bed; Clayton's location had been discovered and he'd already been hauled off by the authorities; Clayton was sleeping peacefully on the bed; Clayton had slipped away in search of Frankie Hilton.

She was prepared for almost anything.

Almost.

Chapter Seven

"Oww!" Tory managed to get the syllable out on the last breath to leave her body.

She fell onto the bed with Clayton tumbling on top of her. Somehow he had managed to trap her hands in only one of his own, so she was forced to buck her body against his crushing weight.

He groaned slightly before rolling off to the side. She sucked in a deep breath and yanked her hands free. "What are you doing?"

"I didn't know it was you," he admitted, sounding apologetic. He reached over her and turned on the light. His expression immediately darkened. "What the hell happened?"

His hand went to her throat, and Tory stilled as his large fingers traced the sore spot where the intruder had tried to strangle her. His mouth became a taut line and his brow furrowed deeply as he examined what she guessed was a pretty decent welt.

"Who did this?"

She told him about the attack in her apartment. Try

as she might to corral her emotions, it was impossible. She felt battered and defeated.

Clayton held her chin in his palm as his thumb reached up to wipe away each tear as it spilled. "I'm sorry you were hurt and scared," he said softly. "Any idea who the guy was?"

She managed a small smile. "I don't have the first clue. But he sure knew me." She told him all about the name thing.

"He wasn't at all familiar?"

She nodded, pushing herself upright and leaning against the headboard. "Very."

His eyes narrowed, but he seemed pleased at that detail. "How so?"

"He was the second guy to break into my home in the same day."

Sitting on the bed beside her, Clayton offered a crooked half smile. "You lead an exciting life."

"No," she insisted as she reluctantly shrugged out of reach and slipped off the bed to stand. She rubbed her arms and silently willed her heartbeat back to a normal rhythm. "I lead a very quiet, sedate life. Boring, but right now that's sounding pretty good to me." She twisted her hair into a makeshift ponytail then twisted it again into a bun. "And to think I was trying to figure out some way to spice up my life." She smiled awkwardly. "Only goes to prove that you should be very careful what you wish for."

He returned the smile, though there was no real humor in his eyes. "Don't I know it. That's one of the things that got me into trouble. Not that I ever wanted

Pam to die, but if I'd kept my temper, I might not have gone to jail."

Tory was too tired and too emotionally drained to beat that dead horse again. What she needed was a relaxing bath and something to eat.

"What do you want to do?" Clayton asked.

"Turn the clock back to when I was a normal, albeit dull, woman?"

Clayton laughed. It was a soothing sound that seemed to settle over her like a warm blanket.

"I doubt you've ever been dull," he countered.

"But I am," she insisted as she fell into the chair. "Until today the most adventurous thing I ever did was move to Montana."

"That's adventurous?"

She smiled. "It is when you've spent your entire life in the same state, in the same county, in the same house."

He shrugged. "Nothing wrong with that. But change can be good."

"That's what I told myself," she agreed. "Only, the change was too drastic. Then the trial happened and I became a pariah."

"I know the feeling. Things didn't work out too well for me, either."

Tory cringed at her thoughtlessness. "I'm sorry. I'm complaining, and you're the one who's been locked up. Sorry."

He met and held her gaze. "I want to trust you."

Her hand went to her throat. "Doesn't this prove to you that I'm not involved in any way? That I don't know anything about Pam and her money?"

"Could be a very clever ruse."

She threw her hands up and let them fall with a slap. "You're starting to sound like an Oliver Stone script. I killed your wife, framed you, hoarded a large sum of money from an unknown source and then I've lived surrounded by people who shun me at every opportunity with a job where I'm hidden in the back like the bastard at the family reunion, because…?"

He shrugged and let out a long breath. "Shun? I thought shunning died off with the Puritans. Is shunning still possible? I would think shunning could be actionable in the workplace."

"Save me," she prayed under her breath. "Forget shunning. Does that scenario really make sense to you?"

"Nothing has made much sense to me since the police hauled me off to jail." He went to the bathroom and brought her a glass of cool water. "Was there anything familiar about the guy in your apartment?"

"Yeah," she stated pointedly as she took the glass. "It was eerily similar to when I woke up with you standing in my bedroom brandishing a knife." She gulped down half the contents of the glass.

"That was unavoidable," he said, though there wasn't even a hint of apology in his tone.

"No, tax increases are unavoidable. Appendectomies are unavoidable." She placed the glass on the table and rubbed her hands over her thighs. Adrenaline had seeped from her body, taking most of her strength along with it. She was left feeling anxious and exhausted all at once. It wasn't a pleasant sensation.

"We need a plan," Clayton said.

"I had a plan," she countered, annoyed. "I should have stuck to my plan. Then none of this would be happening to me."

His interest was piqued. "You have a plan to find Hilton and the money?"

She shook her head. "Not that kind of plan—a *life* plan."

He offered a slightly comforting smile. "Which didn't include murder and mayhem, huh?"

A chuckle rumbled in her sore throat. Reflexively, she rubbed the place where stocking man had tried to squeeze the life out of her. "Far from it. I had practical goals, thanks to very practical parents."

"Like what?"

She shrugged. "Normal stuff. You know, go to a good college, prepare for a career, eventually marry and have the appropriate number of children."

"Not feeling prepared for this?"

"Hardly," she answered with a wry smile. "I've always done the safe thing. I chose a college I could attend and still live at home so I could save money."

His head dipped in a respectful nod. He figured it would be good for her to talk. The attack had shaken her. He found himself torn over her potential involvement in the catastrophe that was his predicament. If she was simply an innocent pawn in all this, he was indirectly responsible for almost getting her killed.

He didn't want to consider his own culpability. At least not yet. So he said, "I'll bet your practical parents respected that."

"They did, mostly," she replied with a sudden sadness cloaking her pretty eyes. "My mother thought I was too practical at times."

"How so?"

"Well, when the other coeds went to Florida for spring break—"

"You stayed home and worked to earn extra money?"

She rolled her eyes. "No. I said I was practical, not a complete dork. I did go to Florida, only I stayed with a distant relative so I wouldn't have to pay for a hotel room."

"Really cut loose, huh?" he teased.

She pursed her lips in silent reproach. "I had a wonderful time. The beach was lovely. I even met a nice guy who I dated until the end of my senior year."

"You really did take a walk on the wild side, huh?"

It was immediately apparent that she didn't appreciate his taunting. Not that he really cared. His mind had conjured up a marvelous image of her in a tiny bikini on a white sandy beach.

"You shouldn't mock me. He was a nice guy," she commented, her eyes level. "And for your information, he went on to the Wharton School and now runs one of the largest banking software companies on the East Coast."

"You keep in touch?"

"Of course," she answered easily. "I exchange cards, letters and even the occasional telephone call with most of the men I've dated. A lesser-known bonus of not sleeping with anyone is that once it's over, you can truly remain friends. My friend Gayle used to say—"

"Back up a minute," Clayton interrupted, his mind replaying that single portion of her comment over and over. "Not sleeping with anyone? You're talking about college, right?"

Her only reply was a pointed stare.

Sighing and shaking his head, Clayton had to laugh. This was simply too strange. "How could I not know this about you?"

Her stare morphed into an annoyed glare. "Because it's an intimate detail of my life that I didn't share with my boss?"

"You don't have an intimate life," he returned with a chuckle. "Which is very abnormal, in case anyone hasn't told you."

"Gee, no, I've never heard that before," she fairly sneered.

He watched as she folded her hands neatly in her lap. She might have been trying to look the picture of prim and proper, but genetics belied her efforts. Granted, the underlying sensuality was subtle, but it was there. His mind was spinning.

She took in a deep breath, exhaled slowly, then spoke. "My very enlightened, personal decision not to have sex—not that it's any of your business, mind you— is based on very sound reasoning. I didn't want anything, especially an unplanned pregnancy, to sidetrack me from my goals."

"Ever hear of birth control?"

"Ever hear ninety-nine-percent effective?" she shot back. "That one-percent chance wasn't something I wanted to risk. Then there's also my fundamental belief that sex should be a magical experience between two people who genuinely care about each other."

"Very happily ever after."

"What's wrong with that?" she countered, obviously irritated with his baiting. "My parents had a great marriage and I decided at a very young age that I wasn't going to settle for anything less."

"Admirable," he acknowledged. "Not very realistic, though."

"Spoken like a truly divorced man," she said on a very judgmental breath that rankled him to the core.

"You aren't in much of a position to be dispensing relationship commentary."

She shot him a disgusted look. "That's such a stupid thing to say. Just because I haven't acted on my urges doesn't mean I haven't had them, or had meaningful relationships."

For the second time he found himself honed in on only a portion of her comments. Urges. She had urges. He was having one right then.

Raising his hands, he decided it was safer for him if they got off this topic. "I think we should devise a plan."

She thought so, too. And part of her plan was to dig a big hole and jump into it. *Why did I tell him that?* she wondered for the umpteenth time in the past ten seconds.

"It probably isn't safe for us here," he commented.

"I know." Tory began to gather up Pam's credit cards, Rolodex and files. "Public transportation is out. I'm sure they've put out a watch for you statewide."

Clayton went over and turned on the small, antiquated television set. Each flick of the dial clicked loudly as he positioned the slightly bent antenna in an attempt to strengthen the signal. After a few minutes the grainy, rolling picture came into focus.

Chandler Landry's image appeared on the screen. Tory noted the dark circles and a tightness around his mouth that normally weren't present as he delivered the evening newscast on WMON-TV. She felt a deep sense of compassion for him. It must be horrible for him to have to be on camera when the lead story was Clayton's escape and current status as a fugitive.

She glanced at Clayton and saw the pain etched in his face. She noted that his fists clenched as he watched his brother read from an unseen teleprompter....

"...last seen on Highway 12 nearly twenty-four hours ago. The s-suspect may be in a 1998 Volvo. Anyone with information is asked to call the state police hotline number now scrolling at the bottom of your screen."

Chandler was replaced by an attractive woman Tory recognized as the weekend anchor, who continued the broadcast.

"In a related development, police are also searching for Victoria DeSimone, who may possibly have been taken hostage by the fugitive. Neighbors reported a disturbance earlier this evening at Ms. DeSimone's residence in Helena. Police entered the apartment, and sources said they found evidence of a struggle. Ms. DeSimone was the prosecution's star witness at Mr. Landry's murder trial..."

Tory saw her photo plastered on the screen. She sucked in a breath. Clayton cursed.

Clayton turned and met her wide eyes. Anger masked his handsome features, and she could almost see his thoughts racing. He started gathering up the items they had decided might be important. "We've got to get out of here."

She reached out and grabbed his arm. "Wait. This can work in your favor. I can tell the police about the man in my apartment, and you can tell them why Michael Greer attacked you. There is physical evidence of the fight in my apartment, so they'll have to believe us."

Clayton continued preparations to leave. "I'm not willing to take that chance."

"But—"

Tory's protestation was cut off by the door bursting open.

Chapter Eight

Clayton lunged toward the officer, grabbing the barrel of the handgun as they fell crashing to the floor. He was vaguely aware of Tory's screams but kept his attention on the task at hand; namely wrestling the weapon away from the smaller man before it accidentally went off and someone got shot. For a wiry guy, the man was pretty strong, but he hadn't spent four years working out. Clayton was able to roll on top of the guy and use his elbow to deliver a swift blow to his opponent's chin.

"Ohmygod," Tory repeated like a mantra.

Slowly, feeling a sharp burn where he'd been stabbed, Clayton got to his feet, holding the gun between two fingers. Brushing hair off his forehead, he stepped around the motionless officer and started grabbing their things.

"Is he dead?" she asked.

"Of course not," Clayton answered as he tossed the gun into the bathroom wastepaper basket. Turning, he noted that Tory was frozen in place. She seemed numb to the distant sound of sirens wafting through the open door.

He grabbed some of their stuff and shoved it into her arms. "We've got to go!"

"But he's hurt," she stammered.

"That makes three of us," he retorted, grabbing the rest of the items and half shoving her toward the exit. "Move!"

The cop had followed procedure to a T. His cruiser was parked directly behind Tory's BMW. Clayton had to make a judgment call, so, after depositing Tory in the passenger seat with most of the files and supplies, he got behind the wheel and gunned the engine.

The sirens grew louder.

"What are you doing?" she demanded as he gripped the gearshift.

Clayton's response was to rev the engine and send the car slamming into the side of the cruiser. The sound of metal bashing metal was deafening, but the goal was accomplished.

Tory alternated between prayer and fastening her seat belt as he slammed the car into Drive and jumped the curb in order to maneuver the car out of the parking lot. The high-performance car gripped the road smoothly as he drove onto the open roadway.

"You destroyed my car!" Tory wailed as she twisted around trying to see the extent of the damage.

"Couldn't be helped," he replied, checking the rear-view mirror for signs of activity. "You have insurance, don't you? I'm sure insurance will cover it."

"Of course, but the 'How did this accident occur' section will be kind of hard to fill out without sounding like I'm the Bonnie to your Clyde." Slouching back into place, Tory silently tried to organize her thoughts.

"How'd you afford this thing, anyway?"

The unspoken accusation in his tone didn't sit well. Not when she knew that her auto policy didn't include comprehensive. "I used the secret money from Pam."

"I'm not kidding, Tory, I want an explanation."

"I paid for it with my own money," she said, refusing to elaborate, on principle.

"Where did you get the money?"

"It was a...gift." *Let him stew about that.*

Clayton veered off, taking the surface streets that ran parallel to Interstate 15. "If you want me to believe that you had nothing to do with Pam's financial scheme, you aren't helping your cause."

Crossing her arms angrily, she stared straight ahead into the darkness. "I'm getting pretty close to the point in this adventure where I no longer feel obligated to help you."

"I'm not asking for help. I want an answer."

After what she felt was an appropriate term of ignoring him, she glanced over at his profile. "I've already told you that I don't know anything about Pam, her death, her money or anything else. And I don't have to justify anything to you. And since you seem to have forgotten, I was the one attacked in my apartment for my troubles."

"If you're not involved, then I'm truly sorry for that."

"I'm tired of this conversation," she told him earnestly. "The fact that going to prison made you incapable of trusting people is sad and I'm sorry for you. But that doesn't make it my problem."

"I don't need your pity. I need to get to Frankie Hilton."

"So, go," she countered, shooting him a hot glare. "Just let me off at the next corner. I'm done helping you."

"No. You aren't."

"THIS IS A VERY, very bad idea," Tory cautioned.

Ignoring her, Clayton parked the mangled BMW in a small alley alongside a dilapidated structure. The air was thick with the smell of stale beer as she followed him up to the side door of the house. Several ferocious-sounding dogs barked and came racing around to charge the chain-link fence. Instinctively Tory stepped back, not at all certain that the metal could contain the vicious animals. The surroundings were completely unfamiliar to her. She knew from the road signs that they were in the outskirts of Butte. But it was the middle of the night and she was cold, tired and about to meet a convicted forger. Her social circle was ever widening being with Clayton.

The door to the house opened with a loud creak, and an imposing figure let out a whistle that instantly silenced the trio of beasts standing guard at the gate.

"C'mon in," he called.

Clayton started forward when she grabbed a handful of his sleeve. "I'm not going anywhere near Cujo and his clones," she protested.

"Melvin? You want to control the dogs?"

The man scratched his chest just above a large tear in his dirty undershirt. "Baby! Princess! Queenie!" he called. The three pit bulls dashed toward their master. Melvin stepped off the sagging porch and clipped each dog to a secured chain. "C'mon," he called when he was finished.

The dogs whimpered but didn't bark as she followed

Clayton inside the unkempt yard to the house. The house looked as if it had been decorated and last cleaned sometime in the early seventies.

They were ushered into a small kitchen and offered seats at a Formica table with olive-drab Naugahyde chairs. She took the one with the fewest rips and was careful to put as little of herself in the seat as possible.

Melvin was eyeing her with equal amounts of suspicion and lust. She wasn't sure which of those she found the most offensive.

"Strange how life works, eh, Mr. Landry?" Melvin asked as he stuck a half-smoked cigarette between his lips and relit it.

Clayton nodded, then turned to Tory and explained, "I represented Melvin a few times."

"Never got more than probation," Melvin added, as if Tory should be impressed by his luck with the judicial system. "Last time I got pinched, I got stuck with a public defender." Melvin smiled then, closing one eye as smoke curled up from the end of his cigarette. "Ended up doing eight months."

"That's very interesting," Clayton injected. "But I'm in a hurry."

Melvin nodded. The action caused one greasy lock of thinning, dull, brown hair to slither forward over his oily forehead. "I've been working since I got your call. Give me the license."

Clayton held out his hand, motioning for her purse. Reluctantly Tory surrendered her wallet.

Clayton took her driver's license out of its plastic sleeve and passed it to Melvin. He moved over to the light and studied it for a second, then said, "The trick is," he began, "a nice clean edge." When he finished, Melvin indicated they should follow him into the adjoining room.

The experience was something straight out of *The Twilight Zone.* An old, worn sofa and scratched coffee table shared the space with a state-of-the-art computer, printer and scanner.

Careful not to trip on a tattered throw rug, Tory stood silently while Melvin scanned her photograph into the machine. He manipulated the image a little, and then superimposed it onto a perfect template of a Montana driver's license.

A few long minutes later, Tory was holding a pristine new license in the name of Pamela Landry. Melvin returned her original, as well.

"I owe you," Clayton said as he handed Melvin what Tory guessed was a wad of her money.

Melvin pocketed the cash. "You always did right by me."

Tory was grateful that the time with Melvin was over. She would have gone running from the house if she wasn't terrified that the dogs would clamp on to her leg with those sharp yellow teeth in the process.

"See, that wasn't so bad," Clayton said once they were back in the car.

"He wasn't leering at you," she scoffed, wishing she could stop somewhere and disinfect her hands. "Now what?"

"Now we rent a car."

Using back roads, Clayton drove to Bert Mooney

Airport and parked her car in the lot. "Take this," he said, handing Tory one of Pam's credit cards.

"What if the guy recognizes me?" she asked, tasting the fear of knowing she was about to commit her first act of fraud. "If we stick to back roads we can—"

"Vegas is over eight hundred miles away. It will take days if we don't get on the highway. This is the only way. C'mon."

Clayton walked her to the door of the small rental office but remained outside by the newspaper machines as she stepped inside.

The smell of coffee stimulated her brain as she donned her best smile and strode up to a long counter. From an adjacent room, she heard the sounds of a sitcom blaring from an unseen television. Reluctantly she tapped the bell in front of her to announce her arrival.

A tall, lanky young man appeared, stuffing the tails of his uniform shirt into the waistband of trousers that hung loosely from his nonexistent hips. He seemed as surprised to see her as she was to be there. She held her breath as he approached.

"Ma'am," he greeted.

"I need a car," she said in a rush of words. Her heart was pounding a guilty beat as she slid the credit card and driver's license onto the counter.

"Don't get too many rentals this time of night," he said as he pulled out a long form and set it in front of her.

Tory didn't respond. She figured she lowered the risk of being found out if she didn't open her mouth. Using the pen chained to the desk, she committed fraud in triplicate, then swore to it with her signature.

When he swiped the credit card, Tory stopped breathing until the machine spit out a receipt that she was also required to sign.

The young man's brow wrinkled with concern as he took the rental agreement and the credit card receipt and placed them side by side. "There's a problem," he said.

Tory was about to turn and run out the door when his frown melted into an apologetic smile. "You haven't signed your card," he explained. She was too numbed by guilt and fear to speak. "You should do that. Someone could steal your card if you don't."

"Th-thanks," she managed as she quickly wrote her fake name on the back strip.

"Now you've got a choice to make," he said.

Confess to fraud or run? she thought nervously. "I'm sorry, I can explain—" she began.

"My fault," he interrupted. "Actually, I'm supposed to ask you if you want an upgrade before I run the paperwork. I'm new at this."

"You and me both," she muttered under her breath. "The standard car is fine."

He handed her a set of keys and a folder with the paperwork. "It's the blue sedan in spot seven. Is there anything else I can do for you?"

"No, thanks," she called as she hurried out of the office. Relief washed over her.

It didn't last long.

"I ABSOLUTELY WILL NOT!" she screeched.

"This isn't open for negotiation."

Clayton had waited until she'd had a few hours of

sleep in the cramped confines of the rental car before telling her of his plan. She was taking it about as well as he'd expected.

"It also isn't open for consideration," she said.

"I need to know you can't torpedo me a second time."

"Not going to happen."

"It is reasonable, given our history and circumstances."

"Reasonable?" she parroted so loudly that his ears stung. "It's nuts. And it isn't necessary. I've done everything you've asked—including committing a few dozen crimes. But I draw the line at this."

"Draw anything you want. It's happening. Suck it up."

Chapter Nine

Monday turned out to be her wedding day.

In the few hours since they'd arrived in Las Vegas, they had put a real hurting on Pam's credit card. Tory had shopped for clothing and necessities, as had Clayton. They had rented a two-bedroom suite in an off-strip hotel and booked the Little Chapel of Love for their nuptials at seven.

Clayton, freshly showered, shaved and dressed in slacks and a pale gray shirt, was in the sitting area poring over the local telephone directory she'd seen him with when she'd gone out there an hour ago to ask what time he wanted to leave. Tory lingered in her bedroom, nervously reminding herself that marrying Clayton under these circumstances was the lesser of evils.

Am I completely insane to marry this man? she wondered. Not because he was a fugitive, she thought with a rueful grimace.

The reality was this marriage was to be a sham. A way to keep her out of court. But if she was being completely honest, Tory had to admit her own motivations. She too feared a repeat of the horrible experience of being forced to testify, then having her words twisted into something other than the truth. She'd hurt him once, albeit innocently, but still, she wouldn't do it again.

Leaning over the sink, she applied mascara while giving herself a little pep talk. *A tiny, little piece of me probably wants to marry him. How sick is that?*

But the truth was she *had* wondered what it would be like to marry Clayton Landry. And if she was being brutally honest with herself, no little bit of paper would make her more loyal than she'd been during the entire course of knowing him.

If this made him feel better, fine. She could live with that. Hopefully.

"Do this and he'll shut up about not trusting you. He'll find Frankie Hilton, clear his name, then we get an annulment and that's that."

Simple.

Only it didn't feel that way.

Clayton slammed the phone book closed and checked his watch. Tory had been dressing for the better part of an hour. For some reason, that annoyed him more than it should. After all, this marriage was his idea. And a damned good one, in his opinion. The legal system he had so loved had been screwing with him for years. There seemed to be some sort of poetic justice in using the privilege inherent in that system to his benefit. As his wife, Tory was precluded from testifying against him.

"We've got to go!" he called out.

She appeared in the doorway to the bedroom looking a little too much like a bride to suit his comfort level.

Somehow the simple white dress hadn't seemed so bridal on the hanger. Pale silk clung to every amazing curve and inspired every cell in his body. She literally took his breath. The only way he was able to keep himself from walking over and taking her into his arms was to envision a big neon sign over her head flashing the word *virgin* on and off.

"You look...nice."

"It doesn't really work as a compliment if you choke on it," she retorted, grabbing up her purse and stalking toward the door without a backward glance. "Let's get this over with so I can have some dinner."

Clayton smiled, now recognizing her flippant remark as one of her defense mechanisms as he followed her into the hallway and closed the door behind him. "I'm not feeling a lot of enthusiasm from you."

"And here I thought I was hiding my feelings so well."

They didn't speak on the short drive to the chapel. It was every cliché and then some, Tory thought as she blinked against the harsh lights of the giant cupid shooting an arrow at a bright red heart in flashing neon on the brown front lawn.

Once they entered, Clayton gave their names to the small, round woman who served—they soon found out—as greeter, notary and organist.

Patsy, as she insisted they call her, was chipper to the point of being annoying. "Such a handsome couple," she gushed. "You'll want the 'Love Me Tender' package. That includes a commemorative album and photo key chains for the both of you."

"Fine," she heard Clayton answer.

Plastering a smile on her face, she looked up at him and said, "The 'Love Me Tender' package. Can it get any more special than this?"

Patsy reached out and took Tory's hand. "Come with me, we have to get you a veil and some flowers."

"Goody," Tory said as she allowed herself to be tugged into an anteroom done in floor-to-ceiling red velvet. Rose-scented potpourri flavored the air as she stood still while Patsy placed a rhinestone tiara on her head and then fluffed the attached netting to cover her face.

"Beautiful, beautiful," she admired, hands on her ample hips.

Patsy then opened a well-concealed cabinet and brought out a nosegay of pink silk carnations tied with a big frilly bow. Accepting the flowers, Tory was then taken to a staged area, and a photograph was snapped.

"Now, listen at the door for the music."

Tory swallowed the knot clogging her throat as she awaited her cue. She had just enough time to question her sanity before "Here Comes the Bride" echoed though the chapel. She was about to take a reluctant step when the music stopped abruptly.

Good, she though, Clayton has regained his senses, and we're not going through with this ridiculous sham.

"I almost forgot," Patsy said as she reached into a drawer near the cash register and produced a blue garter sealed in a plastic sleeve. She gave Tory a wink, then added, "Slip this on. That takes care of the blue. Your beau said the dress was new, so that's covered." She paused to adjust the tiara. "Your headpiece is borrowed. What about something old?"

Tory shrugged. "Clayton?" she suggested sweetly.

Patsy laughed. "Hardly, he's a fine specimen of a man."

Peering out through the small break in the red velvet curtains, Tory did have to agree. He was gorgeous. Not mildly attractive, not marginally attractive…nope, he was make-me-weak-in-the-knees, curl-my-toes, ring-my-bell, be-still-my-heart handsome.

"He is that," Tory murmured appreciatively. Of course, she'd known that from the very first time she'd seen him.

A headhunter had sent her on the interview. No warning, no nothing. She'd arrived straight from the airport looking every minute of her five-hour flight with a two-hour layover. Her hair was a limp, blond ponytail and her makeup had faded at thirty thousand feet somewhere over the Mississippi. Coffee had dripped on the lapel of her crumpled suit, and her one and only pair of panty hose had a run from heel to thigh.

She really couldn't have looked worse if she'd put her mind to it. Her luggage was due to arrive on the next flight, so it was either go to the interview looking like a fashion disaster, or miss out on a great job opening. As bad as she looked, Clayton had been her exact opposite. Walking into the office, she had actually sucked in a breath when she'd caught her first glimpse of the handsome, incredibly virile attorney.

To this day she could easily recall the way his crisp white shirt had set off his deeply tanned skin. He'd rolled up the sleeves and loosened the knot on his striped tie, but he still managed to look elegant and professional. She had some vague recollection of shaking his hand, but looking back now, she could only remember the way her pulse had stopped when he'd flashed that perfect, disarming grin.

So blinded by the perfection of his chiseled features and expressive eyes, she'd forgotten her own name for a second. Instead of mocking her obvious ogling, Clayton had been the absolute picture of decorum. He glossed over her stammering and didn't mention her ragged appearance. He'd been totally professional and amazingly personable.

Really attractive guys were usually really big jerks but five minutes with Clayton Landry had dispelled that stereotype. He was positively charming as Tory sat through the interview, silently planning a future with him. She'd almost finished picking out names for their prospective children when Clayton stood to introduce her to Pam and utter that ugly word—*wife*.

She'd taken the job and kept her crush to herself, and here she was seven years later dreading that same word—*wife*.

"I don't know if I can do this," she whispered, forgetting Patsy was right behind her.

"If you don't, I will," Patsy teased. "Men that look like him don't come along too often. You marry that young man and then take him home and lock him up and throw away the key."

The State of Montana will probably do that. They'll lock both of us up.

Patsy rummaged around in the drawer again, then pulled out a small tray holding several plain gold wedding bands. "For an additional charge of $79, you can pick any of these rings. If it was me, I'd put one of these through his nose so all the other girls would know he was taken."

Tory selected a ring and pressed it into her damp palm. She had the new and the blue and the borrowed and now a ring. And in ten minutes she'd have a husband. Well, not really.

Clayton slipped his finger between his Adam's apple and the neck of his shirt, wondering if the air-conditioning had failed. What the hell was she doing? he wondered. How hard is it to slap on a veil and come down the aisle? What if she had second thoughts? Maybe he shouldn't have made this a requirement.

The curtains fluttered by the back entrance and he was amazed at the extent of the relief washing over him. Though he only caught a quick flash of one of her beautiful gray-green eyes, at least he knew she hadn't run out. He just didn't understand why. Hell, if their situations had been reversed, he doubted he'd have been so accommodating.

In the back of his brain he couldn't dispel the nagging suspicion that she was somehow involved in whatever had sent him to prison. It would explain a lot. It would explain why she had testified against him. It would explain the expensive car and all the electronic toys. At least as his wife she couldn't tank him in front of another jury.

Wife.

Very scary word. Not the concept. No, Clayton liked the idea of marriage—believed life was enhanced by sharing with a partner. Funny, he'd thought long and hard about marrying Pam—hours of agonizing over the pros and cons.

He shifted uncomfortably from foot to foot under the watchful eye of the officiate, who stood about two feet away. He had noticed a small plaque in the anteroom proclaiming the man ordained by some Internet arm of some unknown denomination. Below the certification of the virtual church had been the requisite license from the state of Nevada.

This couldn't be more different from the elaborate service Pam had planned for over a year before the actual wedding. Every detail had been selected for its overall wow factor. He hadn't given it much thought at the time, but now he realized that that wedding had, for Pam, been about the event and not the commitment.

Clayton stuck his hand in his pocket, then felt around for the ring he had just selected from the chapel's private stock. It was a far cry from the five-carat bobble Pam had selected for herself.

The curtain at the rear of the room opened and all thoughts of Pam were completely forgotten.

Tory walked with grace and elegance up to his side. If she was having second thoughts, he couldn't tell. He was having trouble focusing on anything much beyond the way her dress moved as she walked. Small slits in either side of the fabric gave tantalizing peeks at her very shapely thighs.

The minister—or whatever he was supposed to be called, turned to Clayton and offered a broad smile of anticipation. "Please join hands."

There was a slight tremor in her hand as it came to

rest in his palm. Clayton turned and stared down at her shrouded face. He could hear his own heart beating in his ears, nearly drowning out the minister as the organ music wafted away.

"Let us begin."

Clayton heard her small intake of breath and her head was slightly dipped beneath the sheer fabric. He was torn between needing her to do this and wanting to release her from her promise. Panic welled in the pit of his stomach. He could almost taste his own fear as the man began to read from a tattered piece of paper stuck inside a battered folder.

"Repeat after me. I, Clayton Alexander."

"I, Clayton Alexander."

"Take you, Victoria Donnatella."

He squeezed her hand. "Donnatella?"

"Yes," she said rather defensively.

"Whatever. Take you, Victoria Donnatella."

"To be my wedded wife. To have and to hold, from this day forward, for better, for worse, for richer, for poorer, in sickness or in health, to love and to cherish till death do us part. And hereto I pledge you my faithfulness."

Clayton's mind was spinning by the time he repeated, "…my faithfulness."

He listened as Tory said her vows, amazed at the steadiness of her voice. She was proving yet again that she was a very tough woman.

"The rings?" The minister prompted.

Clayton and Tory placed their rings on his folder in turn.

"Lift the veil," Internet minister instructed.

Clayton felt a little bit like a kid on Christmas morning. Odd that he should feel such anticipation at this awkward moment. Grasping the thin fabric, he peeled back the netting to reveal her flushed face.

His gut knotted when he saw the turmoil in her eyes.

Yes, he knew this whole wedding was his idea. Yes, he remembered how fervently she had argued against it. Yes, he realized that in this century, a marriage could be dissolved rather easily. But, no, he couldn't go through with it.

"Wait," he choked out, barely recognizing his own voice.

Tory's gaze registered confusion.

Sucking in a breath, Clayton knew he shouldn't force this. And he was about to say as much.

"He wanted me to buy a different dress," Tory piped in, accurately guessing his change of heart. This was his bright idea and she was going to hold him to it. "Please, continue."

"Uh, sir?"

She held her breath, waiting for Clayton to respond. If he called the whole thing off she'd be mortified. She'd make the *Guinness Book of World Records* as the first bride of convenience dumped at the altar. How embarrassing was that?

It seemed as if three lifetimes passed before Clayton wordlessly nodded.

She grunted some sort of reply when prompted during the exchange of rings. Then it was time.

Every cell in her body waited, coiled, as the minister gave the command, "You may kiss your bride."

Bracing herself, she wasn't at all sure what to expect.

His hands moved up and cradled her face.

Would it be brief? Forced?

The pressure of his palms against her cheeks only increased her anticipation. All of her attention honed in on his mouth as his head dipped ever closer.

She felt her fingers crush the stems of the faux flowers. She could smell his cologne. She felt the slight calluses on the pads of his fingers as they splayed against her face.

Then it happened. His lips brushed hers so lightly that she wasn't sure of the contact at first. It was a soft, tentative movement, though her body reacted forcefully.

It was as if her lips were connected directly into her pleasure centers. There was no logic, no higher reasoning, nothing to prevent her brain from registering potential pleasure in strobelike repetition. It obliterated everything else.

A sound—something between a moan and a squeal of delight—bubbled in her throat.

She felt him begin to pull away and dropped the flowers on the ground. The thud from the flowers hitting the wood floor barely registered as she reached up and grabbed fistfuls of his shirt. This might very well be her only shot at kissing him, and she was going to get her money's worth.

Virtually on tiptoe, she pressed herself against him and kissed him completely. Her palms slid over the taut muscle encased in soft, polished cotton until she was able to wrap her hands around his neck.

He teased her with his kiss. Alternating the pleasure and pressure. The other people in the room evaporated the instant his tongue tested the seam of her mouth. A wild, frenzied rush of need surged though her body. Her fingers raked up into his hair as she attempted to pull him closer.

Her body was full against his as his hands skimmed the sides of her body, coming to rest at her waist. He tasted of mint and passion, and Tory found the combination utterly devastating to her senses.

It was as if she couldn't get enough. She wanted to taste him, feel him, explore every solid inch of his frame and then do it all over again. This wasn't an urge. It was a need. An insatiable need that…

Went unfulfilled.

He set her away from him. Tory felt like a quivering pile of electrified greed. Then she looked up into his face. His hair was tousled from her rather aggressive behavior, and he wore a smile that was half surprise with an equal showing of simmering passion.

Internet minister cleared his throat.

Tory's eyes widened as she realized how inappropriate her behavior had been. In a chapel, no less. She was surely going to burn in hell.

WITH THEIR commemorative keychains in hand, Tory and Clayton left the chapel as a married couple. She had the pictures to prove it. She was the one in white with the very red face.

"Want to tell me what you were thinking?" Clayton asked once they were back in the rental car headed for their hotel.

Twisting the wedding band on her finger, Tory

shrugged. "I think we can both agree that I wasn't thinking."

He sighed as he yanked free the knot of his tie. "You could have warned me. It's been a very long time since a woman accosted me, so I'm going to enjoy it."

"It was a lapse. Can we change the subject?" she asked, her cheeks burn with renewed humiliation at his snort of laughter. Tory quelled the urge to smack him.

"Not likely," he returned easily. "It was hot."

It sure was. "Don't read anything into it. It's been a while and I was simply responding to pleasant stimuli. As were you, I might add."

"I thought I was quite reserved. In fact," he paused and made a superior little snort that irritated her to the core. "If I hadn't stopped you, no telling what might have happened."

"It was only a kiss," she said. "Granted, it was a very above-average one, but it was just a kiss. Grow up and get over it."

"Not likely, and what do you mean 'above average'?"

"Not the worst, but not the best."

"This is rich. I'm getting scored by a virgin."

"It wasn't a score, it was an observation. Drop it."

A few minutes later, she was thrilled to see their hotel up ahead. The interior of the rental car wasn't big enough for her, him and his puffed up ego.

She was still holding her flowers—mangled as they were—when they stepped into the elevator.

Clayton was whistling. In her current mood, the sound was like fingernails on a chalkboard. The elevator doors couldn't open soon enough.

He held the door for her, then followed her inside the room. Tory kicked off the new pumps she had purchased earlier that afternoon. She should be tired. Exhausted, in fact, but that wasn't the case. She was a pillar of tightly wound nerves. Made all the worse by Clayton's apparently jovial mood.

"Want room service, or would you rather go out before we hunt down Frankie Hilton?"

She cast him a look. "You're a fugitive. Don't you think you should lay low?"

He shrugged and smiled with forced innocence. "It is our wedding night, I suppose we should stay in. Especially now that I know how much you like to be kissed."

"I had one little lapse during the ceremony," she complained. "Are you going to keep throwing it in my face?"

"Pretty much," he agreed easily. "At least, I will until I get a better grade than above average."

Rolling her eyes, she tossed her purse and her flowers on the sofa and walked over to him. Tossing her head back, she said in a measured monotone, "Oh, Clayton, you stallion, you master, you're the best kisser in the whole, wide world."

He laughed and reached out to brush a wayward strand of her hair from her face. "Funny, funny girl."

"Arrogant, arrogant boy."

His brow wrinkled as he met and held her gaze. Tory felt a charge building in the small space between them. It ignited when his arm snaked around her waist and he pulled her against him. Hard.

"I didn't mean 'girl' in a condescending way."

"Okay."

His head loomed mere inches above hers. All she had to do was reach up and tug.

"I was complimenting your sense of humor."

"Okay."

His free hand came up to her face, and his forefinger traced the line of her jaw. Tory felt each breath as it left his mouth and washed over her upturned face. When he shifted his weight, she felt the long, corded muscles of his thighs as they brushed hers. That fire in the pit of her stomach flashed, sending a fierce heat through her system.

His hand dropped to her neck. The fingertip trailed along her neck, dipping lower and lower until she stilled and sucked in a breath.

The pad of his finger was on her shoulder, teasing her at the point where her dress met her flesh. Silently she watched as his gaze dropped to follow his touch. He continued the gentle exploration of her neckline, stopping only when he reached the top tiny pearl button just below her collarbone.

"Your skin is beautiful," he told her, his voice strained and an octave deeper.

She swallowed, not sure she could speak above the lump of need lodged in her throat. "The Italian in me," she rambled. "On my father's side. He was first generation. I think I still have relatives in Tuscany. I...I mean I do have relatives there, I—I've never met them. Well, actually, I did meet them, but I was only two and my—"

He silenced her by placing his finger to her mouth. His

hand splayed against her back as he ran his fingertip across her slightly parted lips. He did it again. Then again.

Tory's knees felt weak. Amazing! This man was melting her bones with one simple touch.

"This is dangerous," he murmured.

"Yes, it is."

His hand stilled as he smiled down at her. "It doesn't help my attempts to be a gentleman for you to admit that so willingly."

"Yeah, well, my self-respect is pretty much shot to hell, as well."

"Then we should get back to the task at hand," he said, though he didn't release his hold.

"Or we could play a quick game of Grade the Kiss?"

His expression stilled. "I don't want to play."

Arrow—dead center—ego destroyed! Lowering her head, Tory stepped out of his lax embrace and briefly considered throwing herself off the balcony.

She stepped back, feeling her way along the edge of the table. "Well then, let's find—"

"Tory?"

Reluctantly she looked up at him through the safety of her lashes.

"I said I didn't want to play because it can't be a game. We both have too much to lose."

Nodding, she forced a smile to her lips. "You're absolutely right. Must be the whole Vegas thing."

"The point of this marriage is to protect me."

"Got it."

"I don't think you do."

She was taken aback by his harsh tone. "I get it. This

marriage means I can't testify against you, should that ever come up again."

"We can't complicate things by…by—"

Tilting her head, she glared him into silence. "We aren't. Nonnegotiable. Period. The end. Geez, you're acting like I was ready to strip naked and have my way with you."

"You were."

Throwing her arms in the air, she allowed them to fall against her sides with a slap. "Dream on, Clayton. I'm the one with a proven track record of not giving in to my impulses. I responded to a kiss, I didn't send you an engraved invitation to sleep with me."

"It may not have been engraved," he conceded. "But it sure as hell felt like an invitation."

Chapter Ten

"Here it is!" Tory excitedly tapped the small screen of her PDA.

Clayton came over to where she sat curled in the chair. After fruitless searches in the Las Vegas and Henderson phone books, Tory had connected her handheld to the hotel's ISP and managed to find an address that matched the phone number Pam had listed for the elusive Frankie Hilton.

"Elder Medical Supply?" Clayton read from the screen. "Ring any bells?"

"Not for me," she answered. Her remark was punctuated by a loud, deep growl from her empty stomach. "Sorry."

"I should apologize," he countered. "Let's grab an early dinner, then head out to find Frankie."

She considered telling him her nutritional needs could wait, and she would have, if her stomach hadn't gurgled a second time. "Something quick," she agreed. "Just give me a minute to change."

In the bathroom Tory slipped off her white dress and put it on a hanger on the back of the door. Using nail clippers, she removed the tags from a pair of jeans and a sweater and then dressed in a hurry. The bathroom sported a large, oval mirror and she didn't resist the urge to check her appearance.

The gold band on the fourth finger of her left hand sparkled in the glass. She lifted her hand and studied the reflection of the wedding band. Not *the* wedding band. *Her* wedding band.

"Mrs. Clayton Landry," she said in a near whisper, pretending to greet some imaginary newcomer.

"Victoria Landry."

She tilted her head and watched the ring reflect light as she ran her fingers through her hair.

"Mrs. Victoria Landry. Inmate number 702."

Shaking away the annoying gravity of what she had done—what she was doing—Tory plastered a smile on her face and went in search of Clayton.

She found him poring over the Rolodex they had captured from his family's ranch. He had pulled several of the cards free and they were haphazardly tossed on the sofa next to him.

He looked up, possibly to speak, but no sound came out of his mouth. Instead Tory felt his eyes roam over her. It was a disquieting feeling. Something that lingered between curiosity and intimacy. His mouth pulled into a tight line as his dark eyes continued to study her. Time virtually stopped, as did her heartbeat.

How often had she done this exact thing in reverse? Her office at his firm had provided an unobstructed view of the conference room and she'd taken full advantage of her anonymous perch. She'd watched and admired him more times than she could recall.

Payback was hell.

"Ready?" he asked.

"Very." She grabbed up her purse. "Do we need these?" She motioned toward the cards he'd separated.

"Bring them along."

They decided on the small steak house on the ground floor of their hotel. It saved having to get the car.

The minute Tory smelled food it became her central focus. As she weaved between the linen-covered tables, she couldn't keep from taking inventory of the other patrons' dinners.

This was one of those restaurants that transformed food into small works of art. The aroma of freshly baked bread teased her as she allowed the well-dressed host to seat her.

Accepting the menu, she immediately began to scan the offerings.

"May I suggest a wine?" the host asked, directing his remark to Clayton as he took the seat across the small, expertly set table.

"We'll have a bottle of Alegrini Amarone, 1998, please."

The waiter was impressed, as was Tory. Her knowledge of wine began and ended in those available at her local grocery store.

"Nicely done," she said as soon as the waiter dashed off.

"And I was afraid I'd be out of practice."

She flinched slightly. "It must have been horrible for you."

Clayton nodded, then began to rearrange the candle in the center of the table. "Prison food doesn't register on the culinary scale."

"I can't imagine," she said. Tory slid her hand across the cool, linen fabric covering the table and allowed her fingertips to tentatively brush his.

He offered a weak smile in return for her compassionate gesture. "I used to take things like fine wine and fresh vegetables for granted. But not anymore."

"We'll get to the bottom of this."

Clayton stiffened against his seat. "Easy for you to say."

"We know where to find Frankie and—" She stopped speaking as the wine was brought, acknowledged, poured, tasted then served. "And hopefully he'll be able to explain his connection to Pam and the mysterious money."

"And why his phone number was listed under your name."

Tory felt a rush of annoyance. Pursing her lips, she gave him her best withering glare across the mood-enhancing, softly lit space. "You can't possibly still think I'm somehow part of the grand conspiracy to kill Pam and frame you. I've done everything you've asked, including breaking several laws in several jurisdictions."

Clayton leaned forward, his face harsh, candle flame flickering in his dark eyes. "Forgive me if I'm not full of sympathy. I probably wouldn't be in this mess had you not testified."

Balling her fists and rolling her eyes, Tory said, "Your righteous indignation is wearing thin. I'm not responsible for you going to prison. You said you wanted to kill Pam, I only repeated it and only because I didn't have a choice. So stop throwing it in my face."

"It isn't that easy." He paused to take a drink of his wine. "I'm still trying to figure out how you fit into all this."

"I don't fit," she reminded him. "For the zillionth time, I don't know anything that can help you."

"So you've said," he returned. "If that's true, then why does almost every lead point right back to you?"

She angrily twirled her ring with her thumb. "What leads? Frankie Hilton is the only lead. And we don't know anything about him."

"You're forgetting the guy at your apartment. There has to be a reason why someone would attack you."

"Since it didn't happen until you crashed back into my life, I'm assuming he went to my apartment to find you."

"Or you do know something else. Something you aren't telling me."

Tory gripped her glass with so much force she felt certain it should have cracked under the pressure. "I'm getting really tired of this conversation, Clayton. For your information, you aren't the only one with a lousy life. In a few short days I've gone from the town leper to the paper wife of a fugitive."

"You can hardly equate our two situations."

"In varying degrees," she insisted, though some of the passion ebbed from her tone. "I could very well get into some serious trouble because of all the things I've done for you."

"I took you at knifepoint, and we're married. That should insulate you."

She rolled her eyes. "Hardly. We both know that being married only means I can't testify against you. It doesn't mean I won't have to answer for my crimes whe— *If* you get caught."

"Then I'll have to keep from getting caught."

"There's a plan. Wish I'd thought of it," she retorted as she lifted the menu and continued to study the offerings.

"You can't blame me for being cautious."

Tory peered over the edge of the menu. "Sure I can." She lowered the menu and met his gaze. "You have every right to be annoyed at your situation. I suppose you even have reason to be a little miffed at me because I was indirectly involved in the injustice that resulted in you going to prison."

"Miffed?"

Ignoring him, she continued, "But we're in this together now and life will be much easier on both of us if you stopped being pissy and started focusing on the positive."

"Which is?"

"We found Frankie Hilton," she told him. "It's a step in the right direction. Like my decision to leave Montana. You have to make up your mind, choose a path, chart a course and—"

"Chart a course?"

"Figure of speech. The point is, once I acknowledged that my life in Montana was basically terrible, I knew I had to move. Start fresh."

"Easy for you to say," he sighed. "You are free to do anything you want. Even if I get to the bottom of this, I'll still be an ex-felon."

"No," she countered honestly, "you'll be an attorney who overcame an incredible travesty, who has firsthand knowledge of the justice system. It will make you a better lawyer."

"Assuming I get to the bottom of this. But I think you're wrong, by the way. Who in Jasper is going to hire me?"

She watched as vulnerability flashed in his eyes. It was an unexpected emotion that tugged at her heart. "I will," she promised him.

"To do what?"

She smiled. "I'm going to need a decent divorce attorney."

He didn't return the gesture. It was stupid, but he felt a pang of annoyance to think they had been married for a few hours and she was already planning the divorce. It was worse than stupid. Of course she'd thought through the dissolution of the sham marriage. She would put this all behind her and move to— "Where are you going?"

"Excuse me?"

"You said you were leaving Montana."

She nodded and he noticed that the action caused her hair to fall forward against her shoulders. He wondered if she knew how beautiful she was by candlelight. Probably not. She couldn't see what he saw. Couldn't know that golden highlights framed her pretty face. Or that the soft light splashed the gloss on her lips with warmth.

"I thought it was a good idea before, now it's pretty much a given," she explained. "I started over once, I can do it again."

"Started over?" he asked.

Her answer was delayed as they ordered. "I left Baltimore without looking back. Montana was to be my great adventure."

"Well, it has been that."

"Oh, yes," she agreed with a laugh. "I did pretty well in the beginning. You hired me, I had a good job, I was adapting to western life."

"Then the trial happened?"

She nodded. "It hasn't worked out. So, I think I'll go someplace new. Maybe the South."

"Why not back to Baltimore?"

She shook her head and felt a sadness tighten her chest. "Too many sad memories."

"Like?"

"My dad died last year."

"Sorry."

"Thanks," she lifted her fork as soon as the salad was served. "That's how I got the car."

"Excuse me?"

"The BMW you smashed into oblivion—I bought it with the money I got from the sale of my parents' house."

"I didn't know that."

"It was just a thing," she sighed. The food tasted wonderful so she spent a few minutes savoring the incredible flavors. "Anyway, I had pretty much decided to make a change and then you showed up."

He offered a guilty smile. "You know what they say about the best-laid plans."

"What about you?" she queried.

"I'm happy being a lawyer, but I don't think I'll ever practice again."

"Why not?"

"Jasper is a pretty small town and—"

"They don't have other small towns?"

He blinked as if she'd just told him the secrets of the universe. "I've lived in Jasper my whole life. My family is there."

"A rich family," she suggested. "Your cousin Cade is a pilot, so you've got the closest thing to a private airline at your disposal. You could relocate and still have easy access to your roots."

His brow furrowed as he seemed to digest her words. "I suppose I could look into other opportunities."

"Sure you could," she encouraged. "You could even work pro bono. Just think, you could travel the United States righting wrongs."

"Sounds like I'd need tights and a cape."

She grinned. "Glad you're so comfortable with your feminine side."

"It's something to think about. How's your steak?"

"Amazing," she admitted. "I can't remember the last time I had good beef."

"Neither can I," he teased. "I wouldn't have pegged you for a carnivore."

"Looks can be deceiving," she said.

"I would have sworn you were one of the salad and water types."

"I burn it, I don't store it, so I'm pretty liberal with my food choices. Besides, I come from a long line of food enthusiasts."

"Like who?"

"You don't have to be polite."

"I'm not," he insisted as he pushed his plate away, his full attention fixed on her.

"My mother was an exceptional cook. Every day I would come home from school to a house filled with the smells of pasta and garlic."

"Every day?"

"Of course," she informed him with great pride. "Red sauce is the nectar of the gods."

"That's wine," he countered, tipping his glass to her.

"Wine is in the red sauce," she explained. "At least good red sauce. This is something you can't get in any restaurant in the greater Jasper area. And it wasn't just my mother. My father was a great baker. I learned to dip biscotti in coffee when I was still in grammar school."

"Sounds nice," Clayton said.

Tory smiled. "It was. How about you?"

He shrugged. "My childhood was loud and rough. Seven boys are hard to control."

"I can imagine," she said as her mind conjured a vision of seven dark-haired little boys with piercing eyes and charming smiles. "It must have been chaotic."

"Violent," he agreed, though she heard the love in his voice. "My folks were strict, except on Shane. He was the baby in every sense of the word."

"He didn't seem like a baby the other night," Tory recalled.

"He was always whining and complaining whenever he lost a fight. Which was a lot of the time."

"Why were you fighting?"

"Because we could," he admitted with a chuckle.

"Looking at someone funny could start an all-out brawl in our house."

"How did your parents cope?" she asked, trying to imagine a houseful of adolescents rolling around in combat.

"Very well," he assured her. "We were close, at least until Mom left."

"Your mother left?" Tory choked, surprised since she had never heard this tidbit of Landry lore.

He nodded, but his expression seemed as if he was miles away. "I guess you never know what is going on in your parents' relationship. I would have sworn they were happy. Right up to the day my mother walked out."

"Your father must have been devastated."

"I guess. He moped around, then decided to go after her."

Clayton paused and Tory felt as if she might burst waiting for him to reveal the outcome. He seemed more interested in swilling the few drops of wine left in his glass. When she could no longer stand it, she fairly cried, "Then what?"

"No happy ending," he supplied rather reluctantly. "At least not yet."

"Which means what?"

The waiter appeared at that moment and after they declined dessert, he scribbled out a check. "Thank you and please come back during your stay."

Clayton and Tory nodded to the thin young man. They charged the meal to their room, which was in turn charged to Pam's credit card.

When they exited the hotel's garage, Vegas had come

to life. Las Vegas Boulevard was alive with flashing lights and throngs of people.

The outline of the mountains to the north held the last shadows of sunlight as night descended on the city. Clayton found himself in heavy traffic as he attempted to steer the rental car out of the mass of activity.

Tory had flipped on the map light and was studying the Rolodex cards. In no time, she saw the same pattern he had discovered. "Why would she have so many nursing homes in her files? And why ones in Nevada, Texas and three other states?"

"Pam wasn't admitted to the bar in those other states," Clayton assured her. "It doesn't make sense."

"Wait!" Tory almost screamed.

He heard her rummaging through the bottomless pit of a purse and could only guess at what she might find in there.

"This is from the library in Jasper," she began excitedly, waving a crumpled piece of paper in his general vicinity.

"I need to be able to see the road," he cautioned.

"Sorry," she stated before launching into the next sentence. "Michael Greer, the guy who stabbed you—"

"I remember his name."

"Do you want to hear this?"

"Go ahead."

"The police blotter said he was convicted for passing bad checks."

"Which is relevant how?"

"He wrote seven checks totalling eleven thousand dollars to Mountain Rest Nursing Home."

"That sounds familiar," Clayton said.

"It should. Pam had that business in her Rolodex."

"Where is the nursing home?"

"East of Helena," Tory answered.

Clayton felt his heart sink. He didn't relish the notion of returning to Montana. Though he was still a felon, he felt safer in Nevada. They were registered at the hotel under Pam's name and on her credit card, so he felt a certain insulation from those assigned to find him. Hopefully Frankie Hilton held the answers and he could return to Jasper with a future.

"I think you want to make a left up here," Tory said. "Go toward those warehouses."

Clayton found himself on a poorly paved road flanked by dusty beige buildings constructed of concrete block.

A mangy stray dog darted out from behind a battered blue Dumpster as he inched down the narrow passageway. It was an industrial area and old by Las Vegas standards. The warehouses touted metal signs with equal amounts of rust and weathering. The roadway was dotted with fluorescent overhead lights that cast a greenish pall over the exteriors.

It was deserted save for a small green compact parked on the opposite side of the street. Clayton stopped the car in front of the hand-painted entrance sign by the next to last building on the street.

They approached the door with caution. The walkway leading to the front door was covered in a thin layer of sand, and the air was thick with the smell of industrial exhaust. He reached for the knob when the door swung open.

A tall man with a shock of white hair and deep-set blue eyes stood framed in the entrance. He had sun-weathered skin and slightly arthritic looking hands.

"We're closed," he said in a gruff voice that held the hint of a northeastern accent.

"Frankie Hilton?" Clayton asked, squaring his shoulders and planting his feet as he'd learned during his years of confinement.

"Who's asking?"

Clayton didn't back down, nor did the man. "I'm asking and I don't like to ask twice." Reflexively, he reached back and placed Tory behind the shield of his body. At least, he tried to. She was stubbornly standing her ground, as well, apparently oblivious to the potential danger to herself should things go south.

The man's expression changed suddenly. His mouth curved into something that fell between a smirk and a smile. But it didn't reach his eyes. Nope. Clayton felt a chill as he saw the absolute lack of genuine emotion in the man's gaze.

"You're Landry, aren't you?"

Clayton knew the perils of reacting rather than acting when dealing with a threat. Better to be the aggressor.

He heard Tory's shrill cry as he grabbed the man by his shirt and rammed him inside the building, not stopping until he had sandwiched the guy against heavy, floor-to-ceiling shelving. "And you're Hilton," Clayton countered, bracing his forearm so that Hilton's movements were restricted by the fear of cutting off his oxygen. "Enough pleasantries, tell me why you sent Michael Greer to kill me."

The smile-smirk remained perfectly in place. "It was business."

"What business?" Clayton asked, punctuating his question with an increase in pressure against the man's chest.

Frankie's head tilted to one side, and he regarded Clayton for a long minute. Finally he said, "Are you trying to convince me that you don't know?"

"Know what?" Clayton demanded. He didn't have the patience for this.

"Let's do this in a civilized fashion," Frankie suggested. "Hey, you've already proven that you can kick my ass. So, I'd rather do this in my office."

Wavering just for a minute, Clayton weighed the situation. Hilton was right. He could and would pummel the guy without hesitation. Though he was tall, Clayton guessed the guy was somewhere in his sixties. Even with the lingering pain of the stab wound as a distraction, Clayton could make easy prey of this guy. And it wasn't just knowing he had a physical advantage. Clayton had four years of pent-up rage ready and eager to exact a little revenge.

"If you so much as twitch," Clayton warned, "they won't be able to identify you with dental records. Clear?"

Frankie nodded. As soon as Clayton relaxed his grip, the older man straightened his shirt and motioned them in the direction of the rear of the warehouse.

Clayton made sure Tory didn't get in the way. He wasn't feeling all that trusting and he wanted to make sure there was nothing between them and Frankie should things get nasty.

Their footfalls echoed through the cavernous building. The shelving ran twenty feet high and at least five times that in length. From what he could see, the business was legit. He spotted cases of gauze, partially assembled walkers, trays, crutches, bedpans and dozens of other items neatly stacked and labeled.

The large room was illuminated by rows of evenly spaced metal lights dangling on sparse cords from the ceiling. Along the back wall, very near the roof line, was a large exhaust fan, blades spinning in a rhythmic whoosh that vibrated the building.

Frankie's red leather boots scuffed along the concrete floor as he led them to the office. It was a twelve-by-twelve room with a large, cluttered desk, several filing cabinets, two mismatched chairs, and a sagging sofa against one wall. Frankie leaned against the desk, reaching behind him as Clayton motioned Tory toward the sofa.

"Don't even think about it."

Frankie stopped with his hand in midair. "I'm just getting a smoke."

"This just became a smoke-free environment," Clayton returned. "Now. Tell me what you know."

"She was good," Frankie stated. "Granted, the scheme wasn't hers to start with, but she improved upon it and made us all a pretty chunk of change."

"Scheme to do what?" he heard Tory yelp from behind him.

He turned to give her a cautioning look when she leaped off the sofa, looking very fierce and determined. Clayton admired her moxy. "I've got it under control," Clayton warned.

Frankie's snicker echoed through the open office door and floated out into the vast expanse of the warehouse. "You don't seem to be able to control your women, Landry."

"Didn't we already establish I can kick your ass?"

Frankie just shrugged. "Whatever. The point is, Pam took a simple scam and turned it into a multistate gold mine. Of course, she used my connections and that was supposed to be worth a twenty-percent cut. There was plenty of money for everyone, even with the other partners."

"Partners in what?" Clayton demanded, running out of patience for the man's lazy ramblings. Frankie laughed again. A derisive little sound that rumbled around in his throat and made Clayton wish he had strangled the guy when he'd had the chance. "Lay it out for me, Frankie. I'm getting bored with you."

"What do you know about nursing homes?" Frankie asked.

"The usual," Clayton answered. "Why?"

"A lot of people die in nursing homes."

Somehow Clayton didn't see Frankie as a hospice volunteer. "What does this have to do with Pam's death?"

"There's a lot of money in death," Frankie waxed poetically. "Pam and her partners knew that. Only, they didn't have a way in. I gave them that."

"A way into what?" Tory demanded.

"Asset disposal," Frankie answered.

Clayton stepped forward and glowered at the man. "Pam was an accomplished estate attorney. She wouldn't have needed someone like you to manage estate assets. I don't know what kind of game you think this is, but I'm done playing."

Frankie raised his hands in mock surrender. "The guy from Dallas started it."

Clayton stilled. Pam had done her undergraduate work in Texas. But that was over a decade ago and as far as he knew, Pam hadn't kept in touch with anyone from those days.

Frankie's eyes gleamed knowingly. "I see I'm back on your good side. Okay. In a nutshell, Pam got herself appointed as custodian when someone with money and no close relatives died. She'd gather up the stuff, fake an appraisal and a sale. Usually for about ten cents on the dollar. She'd do all the paperwork and distribute—"

"A fraction of the actual income," Clayton finished. It was simple and profitable. "Who were her partners?"

"I only know one for sure," Frankie admitted. "His name is—"

Clayton heard the pop and a whizzing sound as the bullet passed by his ear and went directly into Frankie's forehead.

Chapter Eleven

"Ohmygod, ohmygod," Tory chanted wildly as she crouched down in the office, arms over her head. Listening to nothing but dead quiet.

Clayton looked as if he might race out after the unseen shooter, but something stopped him. Half scooting, he moved over to where she sat and pulled her into his arms.

Tory closed her eyes and breathed in his scent. It was familiar—at least more so than being in the same room with a dead person.

She wondered what was vibrating. *It's me!* She was shaking uncontrollably. Clayton tightened his arms around her and whispered something soothing against her hair as he stroked his hand down her back. It took several long minutes for Tory to regroup.

"W-what was that?" she asked, settling her palms against the broad expanse of his chest. She felt the rapid pounding of his heart beneath her hands. He'd been as scared as she had. The only difference was he'd recovered faster than she had. Those years in prison had changed him, she knew.

"*Who* was that is a better question," he started to

rise, but Tory gripped his shirt in white-knuckled fists to keep him with her. Even if it was only for another couple of seconds. He gently disentangled her fingers. "We can't stay here."

"We can't leave!" she cried. "The shooter could still be out there!"

Clayton gripped her by the shoulders and held her so that their eyes met. "I think I heard a door and a car. I'm sure he's gone."

Mouth dry with fear, Tory whispered, "What if he isn't?"

He tapped the end of her nose and offered a reassuring smile. "I'm not wrong often."

"Is that why you've been in prison for four years?"

He gave her a half smile that didn't quite reach his eyes. "I didn't say never."

"I'm guessing a call to the police isn't in the cards?"

He shook his head. "We're on our own. I want you to stay put while I—"

"Don't leave me here!"

He bent and brushed his mouth against her forehead. "Don't worry," he said against her skin. "I just want to make certain that the shooter is gone."

She resisted grabbing fistfuls of his shirt and clinging on for dear life. "But we should stay together. Haven't you ever seen a horror movie? It doesn't usually work out too well for the one left behind with the dead guy."

"That's fiction. This is real."

"I figured that out when Frankie stopped breathing."

Lifting each of her hands in turn, Clayton placed a kiss

in each palm and then helped her up onto the sofa. After placing her hands neatly in her lap, he stood and moved over to where Frankie lay crumpled across the desk.

"What are you doing?" Tory asked horrified. "You're not supposed to move a body before the police—"

"You want him looking at you while I'm gone?"

"N-no."

"Okay, then." Respectfully, Clayton moved the man's body down to the floor, then covered his face with the jacket that had been tossed on the back of the chair.

"If I'm not back in five minutes, call the police."

"That's a plan," she rubbed her arms as he disappeared out into the warehouse.

She looked around the small, untidy office. Well. She could either sit here for the duration wringing her hands and feeling terrified or she could do something.

She rose and headed to the file cabinet across the room.

CLAYTON ZIGZAGGED his way through the warehouse, careful to keep to the shadows. He felt his heart pounding as adrenaline surged through his system. Who was the shooter? And how had anyone known that he and Tory would be seeing Frankie. Was their visit related to the shooting, or just bad timing? Frankie had interests outside the law, and anyone in his line of work had enemies. And at any other time Clayton would've dismissed this incident as a coincidence. Unfortunately he wasn't paranoid.

Everyone was after him.

Right now he didn't believe in chance. As far as he was concerned everything circled back to his incarceration.

Reaching the front of the building, he stilled and listened. Muffled sounds from the nearby roadway filtered in, but he detected no sounds of the guy who had silenced his only lead.

His heart stopped pounding long enough to sink into his feet. Now what? he wondered. Frankie Hilton was his best lead.

"Try my only lead," he grumbled as he moved to the door and cautiously opened it just a hair.

The street was deserted. Completely. The small green sedan was gone. Clayton wished he had paid more attention to the lone vehicle. The best he could manage was that the car had been a late-model import, something Japanese maybe?

Turning back to where he had left Tory, Clayton's foot struck something. He heard the scrape of metal against the concrete as the object skittered beneath one of the tall shelving units and disappeared into the dark, cobwebby space.

He was more careful as he made his way back to the office. Tory was waiting for him, her hands full of file folders as she stood over the opened cabinet.

"I've narrowed it down to nursing homes in Montana and Texas."

Clayton stepped over Frankie's body and went to stand at Tory's side. Looking over her shoulder, he turned his attention to the document she'd been scanning.

He noticed two things right off. Frankie had lousy handwriting, and Tory smelled like flowers. The former wasn't much of a breakthrough, but the latter was distracting. He was in the middle of a crime scene and he was focused on the hint of perfume teasing his senses.

And it wasn't just her perfume. His attention was drawn to the gentle slope of her neck visible above the collar of her lavender sweater. The light-colored fabric set off her dark, exotic complexion and only reminded him of her beauty. Closing his eyes, he could easily summon the image of her stunning face. And that incredible body. He needed to concentrate on something other than his companion.

Well, not companion. Wife. His wife.

"…are you listening?" she prompted.

"Sorry," he muttered, rubbing his hands over his face. "Any connection to Pam in there?"

"Maybe," Tory answered, juggling the file folders in her arms to pick a specific one from midway through the stack. "Frankie's company sold medical supplies to Mountain Rest Nursing home in Montana."

"Pam did a lot of work for them."

Tory nodded. "And I've got seven other nursing homes here we can cross-reference against Pam's files."

"Frankie mentioned some guy from Texas. Anything jump out at you?"

"Not really, but I've only had time for a cursory glance. We should—"

"Damn!"

She looked at him, startled. "What?"

"Sirens."

Tory frowned. "I don't hear anything."

"You will in a moment." He started grabbing file folders. Four years in lockup had given him exemplary hearing. "We've got to get out of here."

"Wait. I want to look—"

"Now! Run like hell." He gripped her upper arm and started racing through the warehouse. The faint wail of the sirens got louder.

"Go. Go. Go." Their feet pounded loudly on the cement floor as they raced between the shelving, heading for the back door where they'd parked their car.

Tory's breath sounded loud as she ran beside him. She was terrified, as well she should be. Clayton cursed himself for dragging her into this mess as he slammed a hand on the metal door and they emerged outside in the ally.

Clayton cursed again as the shrill wail of approaching sirens echoed through the warehouse.

"Don't stop," he told her unnecessarily. She was running flat out.

They reached their car as the sirens blared. Close. Too damn close. He yanked open the door and practically tossed Tory inside. "Slide over."

She slid. He jumped in and gunned the engine. He was still clutching the file folders. Tory grabbed them from him, and set them on top of the pile in her lap.

"They'll see us."

"You don't have to whisper," Clayton told her dryly, as he turned the corner, viewing the strobing red and blue emergency lights against the buildings as he gunned the car out of the industrial complex just seconds before they could be discovered.

"That was close," Tory breathed as she clutched the folders to her chest. Her face was pale and dewy with perspiration.

"I'm guessing it was supposed to be."

Tory shifted in her seat and studied his profile in the light from the dashboard. "Someone called the police," she accurately guessed. "Someone wanted us to be caught with the body."

"Yep."

She felt a pang of fear and an amazing anger churning in her stomach. "We were set up."

"It would appear that way, yes."

She blew an annoyed breath at the strands of hair that had fallen forward on her face. "But how would anyone know we were going to see Frankie Hilton?"

"I don't have a clue. Have you used your ATM?"

"No," she assured him. "Everything's been charged to Pam's credit card."

"Made any phone calls?"

"We've been together the whole time," she reminded him. "I haven't contacted a soul."

Clayton turned into the heavy downtown traffic, and Tory found herself scanning every face—from the people in adjacent cars to the sea of tourists clogging the sidewalks.

Bypassing the valet, Clayton pulled into the cavernous lot beneath the hotel and cut the engine. He took most of the files, and then they went to the elevator.

Tory was wound up like a proverbial spring. She half expected the doors to open and some faceless assassin to open fire. And she was equally afraid of the doors sliding open to reveal a well-armed SWAT team lying in wait.

"I am not cut out for this," she groaned when the elevator deposited them on their floor without incident. "My stomach hurts from clenching and I'm afraid."

"Me, too," he admitted as he slipped the key card into the lock and opened the door.

Dropping the files on the table, Tory fell into the chair. She rolled her head around, hoping to ease the strain that made her neck feel like a stone pillar. She rubbed her eyes, then pressed her fingers to her temples. She looked up to find Clayton peering down at her with compassion-filled eyes.

This was dangerous. The very last thing she needed was to forge some sort of emotional bond with him. Relationships based on extreme circumstances never lasted.

Extreme circumstances? her brain screamed. That was a tidy way to describe the past few days of her life.

"I didn't mean to put you in danger," Clayton said, his voice low, deep and way too inviting for her tenuous state of mind.

He knelt in front of her, taking her hands. His face was mere inches from hers. So close, in fact, that she felt his warm breath washing over her in comforting waves. The smart move would be to jump from the chair and run screaming from the room. Ignore the depth of caring in his eyes. Pretend she'd never noticed the way his thumb danced over her knuckles. Forget that her eyes roamed over his face before settling on his mouth.

Yeah, that was going to happen. Not!

Tory opened her mouth but only to allow a sigh to fall from her lips. At the same moment she pulled her hands from his and reached up. Cradling his face in her hands, she saw the flicker of apprehension in his gaze and knew it mirrored the confusion pulling at her insides. She could think of a hundred different reasons why she shouldn't do this, but none of them seemed to matter.

Not here.

Not now.

Clayton knew with every fiber of his being that he should stop this before it even started. But knowing and doing were different things. Maybe it was the sensation of having her slender fingers against his skin. Or the feel of her thighs beneath his hands. Or maybe it was the flash of desire he read in her wide eyes. It didn't really matter. He needed to kiss her.

Right here.

Right now.

Clayton rose, took her hands and pulled her to her feet. If he was inclined to stop—which he wasn't—it would have been impossible the minute he felt the way her small body fit his so perfectly. His hands rested at her waist, pulling her closer so that he could feel as much of her against him as possible.

Just one kiss, he told himself as he dipped his head closer and breathed in a taste of her. He slid his palms up her sides until he cupped her upturned face in his hands. Her skin was warm and the softest thing he'd ever felt. He braced himself, half expecting her to reject him.

Instead, Tory stepped closer—as if that was possible. So close, in fact, that Clayton heard himself groan against her mouth. Need, real and palpable, exploded through his system. His mouth crashed down on hers. His tongue pushed between her teeth.

Instead of rejection, Tory responded with an abandon that set his blood on fire. Her body swayed, pressing the soft roundness of her breasts against his chest. Clayton's fingers raked through her hair as he tasted minty heat and explored the warm recesses of her sweet mouth.

It was as if he couldn't get close enough. His heart raced, his pulse pounded, and he struggled to keep control when her fingers danced along his back. His hands explored her shoulders, then moved lower, lingering in the valleys by her spine. He felt every inch, every curve, then slipped his hands beneath her sweater and caressed her heated flesh.

His fingers brushed the waistband of her jeans and he heard the small moan in her throat. His hands moved lower still until he cupped the tight roundness of her derriere. His body reacted instantly.

Dragging his mouth off hers, he nipped and tasted his way down her neck. Her skin was sweet and flushed, and he found the sound of her uneven breathing exciting. That was nothing compared to the little groan she let out as he nibbled her earlobe.

He was so caught up in the bombardment of sensations enticing every cell in his body that he was hardly aware of the fact that she had pushed him backward in the general vicinity of the bedroom. It wasn't until he felt himself falling backward and landing against the mattress that the situation registered fully.

Her hands were everywhere at once as she teetered on top of him. Clayton peppered her with kisses as her fingers kneaded his shoulders. Somehow she managed to get one hand between them, her fingers eagerly pulling at the buttons of his shirt. Too eagerly, he realized, when the sound of fabric tearing reached his desire-fogged brain.

"Wait," he said, gripping her waist and stilling her body.

"Sorry about the shirt," she murmured, each syllable separated by a feathery kiss against his closed mouth.

"You aren't making this easy," he groaned, speaking to them both.

Tory's hips moved seductively and her smile was pure lust. "I was *trying* to make it amazingly easy."

Clayton rolled her off him, then hoisted himself up on one elbow and looked down at her. She was a vision: blond hair mussed and framing her pretty face; sultry, lazy eyes with thick, soft lashes; and that mouth—lips parted and gloss smudged. She was a multifaceted assault on his willpower.

He smiled as he allowed several strands of silken hair to slip through his thumb and forefinger. "You are full of surprises, Mrs. Landry."

"I haven't been called that since we got—"

"Look—" he paused to kiss her forehead and gather his strength. "I know your criteria for having sex is being married, but it would be a bad idea."

She put her finger to his lips. "Really? It felt like a good plan a minute ago."

Grasping her fingers, Clayton reluctantly pushed her hand away. "We can't make this more complicated than it already is."

She chuckled. "What could be more complicated than marrying an escaped murderer?"

He laughed, as well. "I guess it doesn't get much worse than that. Still, I've got four years' worth of pent-up celibacy so you'll have to be strong enough for both of us."

"That might be a problem," Tory said as she rolled away from him and stood beside the bed. Her cheeks were flushed, her eyes bright. She turned to leave and said quietly. "I have twenty-seven years of celibacy to deal with. We'll see who caves first," she agreed easily.

Too easily, he thought as he watched her get up and walk back into the sitting room. It wasn't watching so much as it was leering. The woman had an amazing rear end. Clayton let out a breath and willed his body back to normal. Normal was a pretty relative term for him just then. His life was spiraling out of control, going Lord knew where, and he was grinning like a lovesick adolescent as he watched Tory fiddling with the papers they'd gotten from Frankie's warehouse.

Having Tory with him was making a frustrating and dangerous situation tolerable. No, he admitted as she began to compare the pages with the cards from Pam's Rolodex. Tory didn't make it just tolerable. She was smart, beautiful and one hell of a trouper. And the icing on that cake was the newly acquired knowledge that she was one very sensual woman.

Sensual virgin, his brain alerted. The irony of it made him want to punch something. Fate had an odd sense of humor.

"I've two possible matches," Tory called to him from the sitting room.

Studying Frankie's poor handwriting was far preferable to thinking about what she had done. Well, almost done. Would have done. Still wanted to do.

Stop it!

"Show me," Clayton said, joining her.

Just give me a second to strip nekked! "This," she began, tapping her fingernail against a work order, "is from Frankie's warehouse, and this—" she paused to retrieve the card "—is Pam's." Clayton read over her shoulder. She tried not to notice the way his breath tickled her neck. She wouldn't do anything about the fact that he was close enough for her to feel the heat emanating from his large body.

Nope. She'd be good. For now.

"Cresthaven Retirement Home, Dallas, Texas," Clayton read. When she handed him the second match, he said the name "Mountain View Rest Home," aloud, as well. "Let's keep going," he said, clearly excited by her discoveries.

Tory and Clayton went through everything and came up with eleven nursing homes Pam and Frankie had in common. Eight were in Montana, the remainder were in Texas.

They moved the files to the table and got to work.

They finished just shy of eleven, but Tory felt as if some piece was still missing.

"If all of this is about money," she reasoned, "then we have to find the source."

"Nursing home patients would be the source," Clayton said. "Deceased patients," he corrected. "If we can find the name of one of those patients, we could find out who handled the phony auction and that might just lead us to Pam's other partner."

"How could she take advantage of poor old dead people?" Tory asked. "That's cold."

"Money," Clayton agreed. "It's actually a rather well-thought-out scam. I mean, who was going to challenge her? If the long-lost relatives didn't know the deceased, then they wouldn't know enough to challenge Pam's figures. Hell, they probably thanked her for the found riches."

"Something is missing," she insisted. "Pam went to a lot of trouble to design a scam that was dependent on the random demise of elderly people. Wouldn't you think she'd want something she could more easily control?"

He shrugged. "America is aging. And death is a reality of life."

Tory scratched her head, nagged by the sense that they were overlooking something obvious. Something important.

Clayton rose and kissed the top of her head. "Veg out in front of the television, Nancy Drew. It's late."

He sat on the sofa and clicked on the remote and began surfing the channels. Tory heard his breath catch as the local newscaster spoke over the two photographs filling the screen.

"...Landry, who escaped after killing a fellow inmate, was incarcerated for the murder of his wife, Montana estate attorney, Pamela Landry. Las Vegas police and the FBI are urging anyone with information on Clayton Landry or his accomplice, Victoria DeSimone to call 911. Again, Clayton Landry and Victoria DeSimone are being sought for the execution-style murder of Las Vegas businessman Frankie Hilton. Hilton was shot and killed in his north Vegas warehouse. Police recovered a .22 Browning at the scene. The gun is registered to Victoria DeSimone."

"You have a gun?" Clayton demanded.

Chapter Twelve

"It was in my apartment," she explained. "I haven't touched that thing since my father insisted I buy it during your trial, when I was getting hate mail regularly."

Clayton began tossing their things into bags after he'd changed his torn shirt. "Move, Tory. It isn't going to take the cops long to find us, and I'd really like to be gone by then."

Using the laundry bag, Tory scooped files and papers inside, then yanked the drawstring closed. Grabbing up her purse, she followed Clayton out of the door. They went to the elevator, watching as a series of lights flashed…seventh floor, eighth floor.

"What if the cops already know we're here?" she asked, panic gripping her throat. "What if they're in the elevator?"

"C'mon," Clayton said, dashing toward the stairwell.

Her face had been splashed across the eleven-o'clock news. She was wanted for "questioning." Yeah, right. They'd arrest her first and ask questions later. A shudder traveled down Tory's neck as she followed Clayton down the next flight of stairs.

He'd only managed to get out of jail by *escaping*. He'd been there four years for a crime he hadn't committed.

Oh, God. Oh, God.

Dead body.

Her gun. Probably covered with her prints.

And Lord—her prints all over the *crime scene*.

Means. Motive. Opportunity.

Did she think for a moment they'd listen to *her?* Not in this lifetime.

Tory took the steep steps two at a time, holding the cool metal railing with one hand, strangling the bag of papers in the other. Not that she'd ever had occasion to bolt down fourteen flights of stairs before, but she was amazed at how strenuous it was.

How had her gun traveled all the way from Montana to Las Vegas? How had it shown up at that warehouse at exactly the same time she was fleeing the scene of a murder? Tory didn't believe in coincidences.

Someone had known she and Clayton were going to be in that warehouse at that exact time. And that someone had broken into her apartment, found the gun and followed them all the way from Montana to Nevada.

The question was—who?

And how had they figured out where she and Clayton were going, when she and Clayton didn't know where they were going from one day to the next?

Her calf muscles ached, and the sack had gained about twenty pounds by the time they reached the lobby exit.

"Now what?" she whispered, peeking out from around him as he cracked the door that led to the casino floor.

"We have to go through the casino to get to the garage stairs."

"And we won't be the least bit obvious with all our worldly possessions in tow."

"Hang on," Clayton slipped through the door and reappeared a minute later pushing a baby carriage.

"The fake marriage was a stretch, now we're having fake children?"

He tossed the papers and one of the bags into the stroller and hurriedly covered them with the pale blue blanket. That left two shopping bags filled with the clothing they had acquired during their speed shopping expedition.

"We've got to move fast. I'm sure the woman I liberated this stroller from is going to come looking for it."

"You stole a stroller?"

"Just borrowing it. Just to get us through the casino."

It was difficult for Tory not to run, but the point was to look normal. A typical young family moving through the hotel. She pushed the stroller across the carpeted floor, hating the layout specifically designed to keep people in the casino. There was no direct route. Just the endless labyrinth of chiming, buzzing machines with looping, repetitive melodies.

Stale cigarette smoke battled heavy perfume from a group of dueling grannies who, from the looks of the empty glasses, had taken up residence at the nickel slots. Tory didn't need a game of chance. Her whole life was one big crap shoot, and the odds didn't seem to be in her favor. At least, not until she could get out of this hotel.

Marathons weren't as long as the distance to the garage stairway, and Tory felt as spent and exhausted as any world-class runner when she finally was able to step into the relative quiet.

Quickly they grabbed up their things, and almost as an afterthought Clayton opened the door and pushed the stroller back onto the casino floor. "Let's move."

They jogged down two flights and then pushed into the cool, dank garage. Exhaust fumes hung in the night air as they reached the car, loaded up and headed out.

Tory didn't relax until Clayton turned the car off Las Vegas Boulevard. The road was little more than a ribbon stretched across a barren landscape. The moon hung low in the night sky, casting long, dull shadows that spilled from the slopes of the far-off mountains surrounding the highway.

"Road trip to Dallas?" she asked as she settled against the seat.

"Safer than going back to Montana, don't you think?"

She nodded. "But drive carefully. Have you ever noticed how many felons get arrested for bad driving?"

"Try and get some sleep. I'll wake you up when my eyes glaze over."

Just before dawn, about four hours and precisely 252 miles later, Tory opened her eyes to a completely different world.

Sluggishly she took in the rugged mountains, deep canyons and the thick forests of pine and fir that rimmed the roadway. She rubbed her arms, also noting the distinct drop in temperature.

"Welcome back," Clayton greeted, his tone annoyingly chipper.

"Is there coffee in my future?" she asked, slapping the visor down in a useless attempt to block the blinding light. They were driving directly into the sun.

"Sign said there was a diner up here about three miles."

Stretching, flexing and arching her body, she tried to work out the muscle cramps from sleeping curled up in the car seat. "You've got to be exhausted."

"I'll eat, then grab a few hours of sleep while you drive."

Fair enough. She could rally. So long as she found some coffee.

As promised, the trees parted to reveal a small, rectangular building off to the right. A half-dozen pickup trucks littered the gravel lot. Tory stood on stiff legs when she got out of the car. Clayton twisted and bent, then gulped in deep breaths of frosty morning air.

The Coconino Café was little more than a converted trailer. Inside the door was a long, polished counter with barstools mounted every few feet. To the left, several roughly carved booths lined the wall. It could have been a cave and Tory wouldn't have cared. Her focus was directed toward the twin towers of coffee urns behind the counter. She wanted to walk over, put her mouth under the tap and open the flow, but instead she settled for a seat at one of the booths.

The waitress was a pleasant woman, with a ready smile that reached her eyes. She wore a pink uniform, faded from too many washings and worn from too many shifts. Pulling a pencil from the pocket of her apron, she asked, "Coffee?"

"Please," Tory answered.

"Need menus?"

Clayton glanced at Tory, then said, "Probably not. Do you have a special?"

"Two eggs scrambled, bacon, toast and hash browns."

"That'll do," Clayton told her with a smile.

They had been together so much of late that Tory almost forgot how very potent that smile of his was. The waitress was still beaming as she moved off to fill their order.

"You have an obscene amount of charm," Tory opined.

Clayton arranged the mismatched utensils on the table in front of him, using the slightly bent knife to cover the flower someone had carved into the smooth surface.

Tory latched on to the steaming mug of coffee the second it was placed in front of her. It was good, hot and washed away the fog of fatigue after a few swallows.

"I thought charm was a good thing."

"It is," she agreed.

"So why does my having it annoy you? You're frowning, by the way."

Tracing the rim of her mug, she dropped her gaze. How was she supposed to answer that? "Ignore me. I need at least a pint of caffeine before anything useful comes out of my mouth."

Tory glanced around, scanning the faces of the other patrons. There were several men dining alone, faces plastered inside newspapers. An older couple occupied the booth opposite them. They ate quietly, speaking only to ask for a condiment to be passed. They had that comfort and familiarity often cultivated during a lifetime together. Tory tried to imagine herself fifty years from now. Nothing came to her.

Breakfast was uneventful, and all too soon she was driving east through Arizona, into New Mexico. One word aptly described the Southwest—brown. The ground was brown. The rocks were brown. The buttes were brown.

The houses, which were few and far between save for those brief times when the highway took her through a town, were brown. With brown roofs and brown landscaping.

She glanced over at Clayton, catching glimpses of him as he slept in the seat next to her. Though her muscles screamed for her to stop, she wanted him to get as much rest as possible. The antibiotics Chance had supplied obviously halted any infection from taking hold, but that didn't mean his body didn't need time to heal.

She yanked the wheel, narrowly avoiding a squirrel with suicidal tendencies. At least, she thought it was a squirrel. It was furry. It had a tail. Close enough.

Clayton stirred but didn't awaken. To the monotonous hum of the wheels, Tory allowed her mind to wander. He did have charm. And intelligence. And amazing good looks. In the midst of this horrible situation, Tory realized she was more alive than she'd been in years.

Being with Clayton was exciting—and not just the dangerous stuff. Of course she was sorry two people were dead, even if they were scummy, bad men who probably didn't add anything to society. But something more had happened.

It was as if she'd reached a destination. Hit her mark. Grabbed the brass ring. Whatever she wanted to call it, she no longer had that rudderless feeling of loneliness.

Nope, loneliness pretty much went out the window five seconds after Clayton had kissed her. Or more accurately, she had kissed him.

"I would have stopped," she whispered. *Right? Of course I would. Maybe I would have. No, I definitely would have. Right?*

Tory sighed heavily, wondering why an issue that had long ago been resolved now seemed so troubling. She was sure in her convictions. Sex without commitment wasn't something she wanted. Not then and not now. Abstaining had never been so difficult before.

She glanced down at Clayton. His handsome, peaceful face stole her breath. Well, *maybe* now.

Do you know how stupid that is? her sanity challenged. Of all the complicated, can't-possibly-turn-out-good situations, this was the hands-down winner. Even if they figured out who killed Pam and why they framed Clayton and shot Frankie Hilton, there was still the glaring truth that theirs was a union born of extraordinary circumstances that would and could never be duplicated. It wasn't as if when this was all over she and Clayton could start from scratch.

Knowing that—even recognizing it with absolute clarity—didn't seem to prevent her from feeling the first stirrings of…what? Love? Now, that would be a catastrophe. How pathetic would she be if she allowed herself to fall in love with him under these circumstances?

Then again, how could she not? In all honesty, she had probably loved him for a long, long time. Maybe from the very start, that first introduction.

But she had nipped those feelings in the bud. He'd been married then. Married men were absolutely off-limits.

Then he'd split with Pam and, even though she still found him incredibly attractive and she was drawn to him almost instinctively, she did nothing. He was on the rebound then, and men on the rebound were off-limits, too.

Then came the trial, her testimony, his sentence and his vocal anger. No room in any of that for fostering a relationship. And even though she'd written to him a couple of times, his lack of response had been enough to convince her to simply go away.

It wasn't as if this latest encounter had started off on the best foot, either. He'd kidnapped her at knifepoint, for heaven's sake. Dragged her into lethal situations, coerced her into committing crimes, forced her to marry him, and here she was chauffeuring him through the southwestern U.S. "How big a fool am I?" she whispered.

Huge. Because at the end of the day, Tory knew there would always be a part of her that cared for Clayton. If she wasn't careful, she'd end up being her own worst enemy.

His butt was numb from the long drive. He guessed Tory was equally relieved when he pulled into a small motel on the outskirts of Dallas. Though she hadn't complained, it had been a long, arduous drive.

Gray fast-moving clouds darkened the afternoon sky as they parked and went into the office of the Lazy D

Motel. Technically, it was an "otel" since the *M* had fallen off the sign and was now braced against the post.

A teenage boy wearing a dress shirt three sizes too big looked up from a computer screen when they walked in. "Afternoon," he greeted, pausing the video game before stuffing his shirttails into his jeans.

"We need a room."

"For the night?" The kid was speaking, but his full attention was on Tory.

Clayton stood for a minute, thinking the young man would remember his manners. He thought wrong. The kid all but drooled, his narrow brown eyes following Tory as she went to the vending machine for a soda. This teenager was ogling her fanny! For some reason, probably because of the long drive, Clayton felt a strong surge of annoyance.

"If you can stop staring at my wife's ass, yes, we'd like a room."

"S-sorry," the teenager said, and then he fumbled with a registration form.

When Tory came over, Clayton felt possessed to clamp his arm around her shoulder. It was an idiotic, childish move solely and only designed to show the young man that Tory wasn't available. Forget that Tory wouldn't have been interested. Forget that the kid was probably so naive that he'd choke on his own tongue before being able to converse with a living, breathing woman.

Nope, Clayton's actions harkened back to a time when his ancestors fell from the trees. It was a juvenile, archaic display of superior testosterone. But it was his testosterone rush, and so he went with it.

Since they were using Pam's credit card, Tory filled out the application, requested the largest room available and then signed the form. Peeping Teenager gave them the key to room six and a sheet of paper that had obviously once served as a place mat, but contained maps and directions for area restaurants.

"We can get two-for-one corn dogs at Happy Harry's Wieners if we order before six," Tory said after he had unloaded the car. "There was a coupon book by the vending machine."

"I didn't notice," he commented.

She was watching him intently from her comfy sprawl on the closest of two double beds. "What was that whole arm-around-me thing at the registration desk?"

"The kid was undressing you with his eyes." He heard her laughter and it didn't sit well. "That's funny?"

"He was what? Sixteen. He probably doesn't know how to undress me with his hands."

Clayton shrugged. She was most likely right about that. The Lazy D Motel was just off the beaten path enough to be a vast wasteland to an adolescent. The teenager probably didn't see too many women, let alone striking blondes with brilliant eyes and olive skin.

"So are you telling me that you want corn dogs?"

"Not really. I was just trying to save some money. Speaking of which. We should go someplace and get a cash advance on this credit card. After the wedding, two meals on the road and several vending machines, our cash situation has reached critical mass."

"There was a grocery store back a couple of miles."

She smiled. "No cameras at the cash machines. Very smart."

"What's the point of being a criminal if you can't utilize your criminal mind?"

She tossed a pillow at him—which he caught easily. "I need a long soak in the tub. I'm stiff."

"Do that," Clayton agreed. "I'll go get the cash and grab a few necessities from the store. Is an hour okay?"

She nodded, then rolled up to a sitting position and reached for one of the bags. "I'm glad we had our shopping spree before we were run out of town."

"I'm glad you're happy. I'm just thrilled to have something that isn't orange."

"I can understand that," she mused, selecting a frilly silk skirt and a matching sweater from the bag. Tory found her toiletries and undergarments, then headed into the bath.

The small room was clean, but that was about the only positive. A large, brownish rust stain trailed from the faucet down to the rubber stopper chained to the hot water lever. The floor was cold beneath her feet, and she stubbed her toe against one replaced tile that didn't quite fit its assigned spot.

Luckily for her the water ran hot, so she poured an herbal additive into the stream as steam began to fill the room.

After wrapping her hair in a thin but functional towel, she climbed into the tub and let the warm water massage her stiff body. She spent the better part of the next forty minutes adding hot water to her tub. By the time she dried off and dressed, she felt like a new woman.

The motel room was dark until she stumbled to the

nightstand and found the switch on the lamp. Cautiously she opened the edges of the curtains and glanced into the parking lot. A small car was pulling out of the lot, but there was no sign of Clayton.

Nervously she checked the clock. What if he'd been captured? Or killed?

Her stomach knotted.

She should have insisted he take her cell phone.

Tory paced, barefoot, at the end of the beds. She should have gone with him. Maybe she should turn on the television. Surely it would make the news if Clayton had been caught.

It was past time for the evening newscast, and without the miracle of cable, she was limited to different episodes of the same sitcom reruns or gossip from a collection of highly polished Hollywood insiders. She switched the set off.

Hearing a noise outside, she returned to the window and poked the edge of the drape.

Seeing the rental car pull into the parking spot brought instant relief to her clenched stomach. Abandoning pretext, she flung open the door and nearly knocked him down as she ran to greet him.

Clayton caught her with one arm, hooking her into a hold and lifting her off the ground. She kissed his lips and hugged him hard.

"Nice welcome," he said, kissing her back with interest. "I can go out and come back again."

Tory slid down until she felt the ground beneath her toes. "You were gone a long time and I got worried and—" she licked her lips "—did you have a beer?"

He smiled and nodded. "A very cold, very good beer." Opening the back seat, he retrieved a bag with the grocery chain's logo.

Tory frowned. "You shouldn't be drinking and driving."

"I was drinking and sitting," he corrected, grinning. "I wanted to get a look at Cresthaven, so I drove over there."

"And?"

Clayton's face practically beamed. "We've got a meeting in two hours."

"With the director of the nursing home?"

"Not exactly."

Chapter Thirteen

"And a straightforward meeting with one of the administrators wasn't possible because?" Tory asked, stepping from the car.

"I didn't want to risk having to give our names," Clayton explained, placing one large hand at her back. "Besides, one of the first things you learn in prison is how to circumvent authority."

Apparently this clandestine meeting was to take place in a small public park about a mile from the nursing home. Clayton led her toward a cluster of picnic tables situated in a clearing. Her eyes darted around, searching the perimeter of the clearing for signs of the man who'd agreed to meet them.

"Does this guy know who you are?" she asked as she stood at the edge of the table. "I mean, does he know you're wanted?"

"Nope. He only knows I gave him a hundred bucks to meet us and I'll give him another hundred if he gets us into the office."

"How did you find him? Was he wearing some sort of sign that said he was available for a bribe?"

Clayton leaned back on the edge of the table, then lifted a foot onto the attached bench. His hands were stuffed in the front pockets of his jeans.

Even in the dim shadows from a far-off streetlamp, he was brilliantly attractive. Tory reminded herself that they were there on a mission. This was not the time to be noticing his long muscular legs. Or the woodsy scent of his cologne.

"I took a chance," he answered. "I waited outside until I saw someone wearing a wedding ring and an old uniform."

She gaped at him, but his attention was fixed on scanning the area for signs of their contact. "Why would those two things convince you he'd take a bribe?"

"Orderlies wear uniforms and don't make a huge salary. Married orderlies probably have children, therefore—"

"The person would be more open to taking money under the table," she finished. "But you have no guarantees that he'll show up. Or if he does, you would have no way of knowing that he won't turn us in."

"You've got to take chances in life," Clayton replied, his voice calm and his manner completely at ease. At ease, but certainly aware. His eyes moved about constantly, tracking the slightest movement, obviously alert to every sound. Tory wondered what it must be like to have to live like that. On edge. Alert at all times. Waiting for something bad to happen. Oh, God, she thought biting back a groan. She was doing the same thing.

She felt as though she had a permanent target painted on her back. Her nerves stretched a little more as she scanned the dark trees nearby for any sign of movement.

She was a bundle of coiled apprehension. Not that this was a new feeling. Relaxation wasn't a component of running from the law.

Beams from car headlights sliced through the dark as a car pulled into the lot. The engine coughed and died slowly, filling the air with a thick stench of burning oil.

The person who started toward them couldn't have looked more harmless. Tory guessed he was young—barely voting age. His thick, curly brown hair looked a lot like a frizzy football helmet. He walked quickly, taking strides that pushed the limits of his short, stocky legs.

When he reached them, he didn't stop moving. Instead, he shifted nervously from foot to foot, then sniffed and wiped the back of his hand across his nose.

"Nice to see you again, Jerry," Clayton greeted.

"Got my money?"

Tory inched closer to Clayton, alternating her attention between the skittish young man and the parking lot.

"Depends on what I'm buying."

Jerry pulled a crumpled piece of paper from his pocket and unrolled it. Next he handed Clayton the paper and the single key that had been curled inside. "There's a shift change at eleven. The RNs and LPNs hang out in the break room for at least ten minutes. There's no night custodian, so you shouldn't have too much trouble getting to the office. I drew you a map. Just make sure you take the west hallway."

"You aren't coming with us?" Tory asked, suspicious.

Jerry shook his head. "No way. I made a copy of my master key. That'll get you in every room in the building except the pharmacy. Only the charge nurse and the docs can get to the drugs. My money?"

Clayton handed him a crisp bill.

Jerry was about to walk away when Tory reached out and pinched hold of his shirtsleeve. "You didn't tell anyone we'd be coming, right?"

"Jerry wouldn't be that dumb," Clayton commented, his voice steely. "I already told him I'd made a record of the serial number from the hundred I gave him."

"I never met you, man," Jerry insisted. "Can I go now?"

Tory let go of him and he hurried back to his disintegrating car. The engine cranked three times, sputtered, coughed up some bluish smoke, then rumbled to life.

"Let's get going," Clayton suggested. "I already scoped out a place to park near the nursing home. Easy in. Easy out."

"Let's hope so," Tory grumbled.

As promised, Clayton parked in a residential section around the corner from the stately old mansion that had been converted to its present use. Other than the sign planted in the front lawn, it could still be a massive private residence built with great attention to detail in 1901.

It was an old Victorian, with two-story covered porches and a front walkway with an elegant circular fountain surrounded by neatly trimmed boxwoods. Landscaping lights shone up from inside hedges, bathing the pale yellow building in soft, complementary light.

"I could be happy growing old in a place like this," Tory commented as they approached.

"Got seventeen grand a month?" Clayton countered.

"That's what it costs?" she cried softly, astounded.

After a quick mental calculation, she said, "That's more than two hundred thousand dollars a year! Who can afford that?"

He chuckled softly. "People with good insurance or great savings."

Using the side door as Jerry had instructed, they slipped inside without incident. Tory's heart raced as they crept slowly down the hallway. Dim wall sconces illuminated the cream-and-burgundy-striped wallpaper and small half-round tables cluttered with kitschy items and silk flower arrangements. The still air smelled of pine cleaner, rose air freshener and old age. They came upon the first door. It was opened enough so that she could see into the room. A shell-shaped night-light illuminated the room's occupant. A frail woman was asleep in the bed, surrounded by machines and IV poles. Granted, the decor had a decorator's touch, but in the end it was still a glorified hospital room.

They passed three more rooms before Tory heard the muffled sounds of laughter up ahead. She froze—convinced they'd be discovered at any moment.

The voices were coming closer. Thinking quickly, she reached back and turned the knob. With the door opening, she grabbed Clayton's hand and yanked him in with her.

She managed to close the door without a sound and leaned against the cool, polished wood to listen.

Two women—who she assumed were staff members—were having a very lively discussion about someone named Melvin. Apparently Melvin was dating someone named Carol. Carol didn't know that Melvin was also dating someone named Beth. Beth did, however, know about Carol. But Melvin didn't know that Beth had dated everyone within the greater Dallas area.

It was obvious by the tone and volume that the women had stopped just outside their door. Tory tasted her own fear. What if they came in?

She didn't have a chance to think of an answer. She was suddenly flying through the air, then sliding until her head tapped something cold and round. The bed frame. They were under the bed!

She would have cried out except that Clayton had managed to clamp his hand over her mouth. The door opened. Tory saw two sets of feet in the pie-shaped slice of light from the hallway.

"Time to check your sugar, Mrs. Patterson," one of the nurses said. Screamed actually.

"She can't hear you, girl," the other nurse commented. "Just stick her crippled old finger and move on."

Reaching up, Tory placed her hand over Clayton's, wordlessly letting him know that she wasn't going to make a sound. Silently, though, she was damning the heartless nurse to hell.

They waited for a full minute after the white shoes had squished out of the room before they emerged from under the bed.

Tory couldn't help herself, she checked on Mrs. Patterson, who appeared to be sleeping soundly in the bed. One of the woman's arms was on top of the covers, so Tory carefully lifted the feeble arm and tucked it under the warm bedspread.

"Remind me to put aside enough money for my first

daughter to go to college and get that geriatric nursing degree," she whispered before they continued on their quest.

He shot her a glance. Yes. He could imagine Tory with a child. A little girl with her silky hair and sparkling eyes. He frowned. Whose child would she be? Who would Tory pick as the father of her children?

Not a freaking ex-con. That was for sure.

He took her hand and pulled her down the hallway behind him. He didn't give a damn that there was enough light to see by. He wanted to feel her slender hand in his. Needed the connection.

He was relieved when they didn't encounter any other employees on their way to the administrative office.

Suite, actually. They went through a sitting area with a small sofa and an ornately carved desk and chair. Everything was neat and tidy. Hopefully that would work to his advantage. He reluctantly released Tory's hand so they could both search.

Jerry had specifically said that the files were in a converted closet through the main office. He'd start there.

"What am I looking for?" Tory whispered.

"Start with the desk," he answered.

"Okay. Hang on." She wiped a crocheted afghan off the back of a chair, rolled it and wedged it against the base of the door to block the room's light from alerting anyone out in the hallway.

"Smart thinking," Clayton said, turning back to the closet.

The files were indexed by year and referenced alphabetically. Nothing under Landry. Nothing under Pam. Nothing obvious. Shame.

Not knowing exactly what he expected to find, he took his cue from the filing system. He tabbed through the first drawer and still didn't understand the color-coded dot stickers attached to each file. There were two colors—blue and yellow. The yellow dots were rare, but that eliminated gender as the basis for the code. He scanned the personal sections and disregarded age as the determining factor.

He'd been reading names, dates of admission and dates of death for the better part of half an hour before Tory joined him in the file area. "I found one of Pam's cards stapled in the address book."

"That's a start."

"And the end as far as the phone book is concerned."

"I'm not doing too well, either," he admitted, frowning. Turning, he saw the Cheshire grin on Tory's face and felt his spirits lift. "But?"

She crooked her finger. "Come with me."

The computer screen glowed blue with file icons lined in precise rows. Tory sat in the seat and worked the keyboard.

"Re the estate of Hedda Blevins," he read aloud. It was a cover letter written by the accounts manager of the nursing home to Pam dated seven months before the murder. "It's something," he admitted.

Tory turned and lifted her face to him. "Meaningless in and of itself, but watch this." She tapped a few keys, making the computer's processor spin to life.

"Eleven other file names that mean what?" he asked over her shoulder.

"All of these—" she pointed to the file names as she spoke "—mention Pam by name."

The knowledge that she had found some tangible link to Pam pleased him to no end. Maybe somewhere in the correspondence was the name of the elusive partner Frankie Hilton had referenced. For the first time in what felt like forever, Clayton felt hope. And he had Tory to thank for that. Impulsively he bent forward and placed a kiss on her cheek. "Now we're getting somewhere."

"Maybe," she clarified, caution in her tone. "All of the letters are the same. Requests for payment of the final bill. And this computer only has copies of correspondence sent in the past five years archived, so anything before that isn't here."

Undaunted, Clayton refused to allow his positive vibe to be dashed. Placing his hands on Tory's shoulders, he let his mind play with the possibilities.

If Pam was the appointed executrix of the estate, it would have been her responsibility to make sure the outstanding bills were paid. His thumb slipped over and lazily stroked Tory's exposed skin.

Her skin was so smooth!

So how did Pam—a lawyer in Montana—end up representing the estate of a woman in Texas?

And soft—very soft skin.

Pam was a member of the Texas Bar as he recalled. He knew from the assortment of Christmas cards over the years that she stayed in touch with some of her old school friends. Maybe one of them sent estate business her way.

His fingertips found Tory's collarbone. She smelled of soap and flowers.

"Can you print the letters?"

"Mmm-hmm."

Those two syllables were soft and sultry. Though he would have preferred to fix his full attention on all things Tory, he knew that would have to wait.

For how long? his libido asked. Anything more than the next ten minutes was too long. He was a pig. A pig with a memory. And how he remembered! Every second of their passionate encounter in Las Vegas was branded in his mind. He knew how she tasted, how she smelled, how her smooth skin flushed with heat. He remembered the desire—the need—the ache. It had taken every ounce of his willpower to keep from taking what she had so generously and willingly offered. He doubted he'd have such strength of character again.

So stop touching her! He was acting like the kid who, upon hearing that the fire is hot, insists on sticking his hand in it to see *how* hot.

She handed him the freshly printed letters, and he returned to the file room. Working chronologically, he started with the oldest and began pulling the patient records.

"It's been eight minutes," Tory reminded him. "I printed out the duty rosters for the past five years. Maybe Pam's partner worked here. Are we stealing those?"

Clayton tucked several folders under his arm. "Borrowing them. We'll mail them back."

"I feel like I've joined the crime-a-day club," she joked, turning off the computer while he picked up the afghan and returned it to the chair back.

Their exit went without a hitch. They arrived back at

the Lazy D in the wee hours of the morning, but he wasn't tired. Not when the answers to his life crisis might be buried somewhere in one of the files.

Spreading the folders out on the bed, Clayton planted himself on one side, Tory took the other.

She had slipped off her shoes and curled one shapely leg beneath her as she fixed that sharp mind of hers on the pages before her. Yet again Clayton acknowledged how incredible this woman was.

After watching her for a few minutes, he quietly called her name. She looked up, the corners of her pretty mouth curved with an expectant smile.

"I'm sorry."

Her response was a quizzical stare.

"I was a jerk for thinking you were involved in this mess."

"True," she agreed with an easy grin.

"I was also a jerk for being angry at you for what happened at my trial."

"Also true." She went back to reading the dry, complicated medical records.

"I was a real jerk for involving you in all this. I'm sorry for everything I've done since I showed up at your apartment."

He thought he saw a flash of emotion on her face before her smile slipped ever so slightly. "Yeah, well, I'm sure you'll make a great character witness at my trial."

Letting out a slow, deep breath, Clayton turned his attention to the records. It was the reading equivalent of watching paint dry. The pages documented when therapies were ordered, given, discontinued. Everything about every medication was carefully listed and initialed. Doctors' visits were chronicled—basically every aspect of the given patient's life. And death, for that matter. All the files had copies of the death certificate.

Clayton tried to find common threads in any number of areas. The patients in his pile of folders varied in age, gender and malady. Pretty much the only common denominator was residency at Cresthaven. Next, he checked the duty rosters against dates and times of death. Still nothing. He checked causes of death.

"Yellow is undetermined," he said aloud.

"What?" Tory asked, rubbing her eyes.

Reaching across the bed, Clayton grabbed up the folder she'd been reading that had yellow stickers affixed to them. "See these?" he said, trying to temper his excitement.

"Some of the files have colored dots on them, so?"

A theory was taking shape in his mind. "Of the eleven estates Pam handled, five have yellow stickers. Those patients died from undetermined causes."

Tory cringed and cast him a cautious look. "That can't be uncommon. A lot of older people die with so many illnesses that I'm sure one single cause of death can't always be determined."

He shook his head. "No. The ones with blue dots all list a specific cause of death. Like congestive heart failure."

She reached out and patted his hand. "These were all sick, elderly people," she reasoned. "Besides, if an undetermined cause of death is the red flag, then all of the files linked to Pam should have yellow dots. They don't."

"Okay," he agreed on a frustrated breath. "Then we're missing something. Maybe they have—"

"Wait!" she yelled, scrambling to take files out of his hand and virtually shoving him off the bed in order to arrange each file in a very specific pattern. One Clayton recognized immediately.

"I'll be damned."

Chapter Fourteen

"Brilliant!" Clayton exclaimed. "All of the estates Pam handled in the six months before she was killed were from people who died of undetermined causes."

Tory beamed. "That seems like too much of a coincidence, don't you think?"

"Absolutely. Judging by the files, Pam took control of the assets, but she wouldn't have had time to liquidate. That must be the money Greer and Frankie were taking about."

"How would Frankie and or Greer have intimate knowledge of Pam's legal responsibilities?"

"I don't know yet," Clayton stroked the faint stubble around his chin. "We've only got part of the puzzle, but for the first time in a very, very long time, I see light at the end of the tunnel."

Smiling up at him, Tory read the gratitude in his eyes. That was all well and good, but it fell a little short. She didn't want gratitude. She wanted…what?

Stepping away from him, she grabbed up the ice bucket and made a quick excuse to leave the room.

"I am such a sap," she grumbled to herself as she

swung the bucket at her side. "What are you thinking, Victoria?" she chided. The situation would end, hopefully with Clayton's full exoneration, and then what?

She stepped into the brightly lit cubicle where an ancient ice machine rumbled and vibrated. Ramming the bucket under the chute with enough force to overfill the plastic container, she felt several dozen wayward ice cubes pelting her bare feet. Cursing, she yanked the bucket away and managed to spill a few more cubes. With her toe, she soccer kicked the ice under the machine so the next patron wouldn't end up slipping or stepping into a puddle of cold water.

Then I get a divorce, move to someplace new and never see Clayton again. Ever. Her chest seized at the thought. Leaning back against the cool, concrete wall, she lingered, not quite ready to face him until she wrangled her whirling thoughts. Not an easy task.

"What are my choices?" Option one—pretend she wasn't attracted to him while she helped him clear his name, then shake hands at the end and walk away with her head held high. Option two—have the guts to force a brief affair and cherish whatever happened for the rest of her life. It was like being on a tightrope and being asked to pick which way she wanted to fall. No, it was worse than that. Both—either—promised a painful outcome.

She was actually warming to the notion of an affair. Technically, she would not be compromising her beliefs. She was in a committed relationship. It was a relationship, and she definitely should be committed!

Tory shook her head, trying to keep the nervous sarcasm at bay. Even between herself and herself.

If only she hadn't kissed him. If only he hadn't kissed her back. If only she could do it again.

Soon.

She returned to the room with ice and no answers. When she caught sight of Clayton, she forgot to breathe. It wasn't fair for one man to be so perfect. He was more than six feet of raw masculinity. That was bad enough, but when he smiled, it only enhanced his appeal.

"I got some bottled water at the store," he said easily. "I didn't know what you wanted."

You. Naked. Now.

"Water is fine," she managed over the lump in her throat. Lots of water. Cold water. Thrown in my face so I'll think about something other than sex. Or the lack thereof, she corrected mentally.

She poured two glasses and brought one to Clayton. As she passed it to him, she spotted the small tremor in her hand.

"Are you okay?" he asked.

"Dandy," she replied, wondering why her tone was so snippy. "I mean, I'm great." Averting her eyes, she moved as far away from him as the small room would allow. It wasn't nearly far enough. His presence seemed to fill the space.

He rose off the bed but didn't move toward her. "What's wrong, Tory? You look…spooked."

Sucking in a deep breath and exhaling slowly, she mustered the fortitude to meet his intense gaze. "I have sex issues."

His lips quivered, and then despite his best efforts, he grinned. "Sex issues?"

She felt flustered and awkward. Might as well just get it out in the open. "Do you think it would be a good idea for us to have sex?"

"It would be a very bad idea," he answered without even a polite hesitation.

Tory felt her cheeks flame and knew her humiliation was complete. "Okay, then. W-well, that settles that." Balling her hands into fists at her sides, she turned and said, "This won't work. We can't stay in the same room together."

Clayton didn't respond immediately. He simply leaned against the wall as if he didn't have a care in the world. "Why not?"

His shirt pulled tightly across his belly and chest, the soft fabric in no way disguising what lay beneath. Her eyes roamed boldly over the vast expanse of his shoulders, drinking in the sight of his impressive upper body. She let her gaze drift down, openly admired the powerful thighs straining against his jeans. If the mere sight caused a fluttering in the pit of her stomach, what would it be like if he touched her. Slowly Tory let her lashes rise until she was looking at his face again.

"Because of this…this…*this* between us." She took two breaths to calm her rapid pulse. "My self-control seems to go right out the window whenever you're around. And you just made it very clear that you don't want me and you think it would be stupid for us to sleep together."

"I disagree. And you're wrong. I do want you, Tory."

"Well, that isn't what you just said," she insisted. "And don't backpedal now. I made the suggestion. You said no. I'll get over it. I'm not a child. I learned a long time ago that in life, you don't get everything you want."

"Is sex what you really want from me? I need to be very clear about what you mean."

Tory closed her eyes briefly. "I mean I'm very confused. It means I'm scared by the way you make me feel. It means I should be thinking about keeping you out of jail and staying out of jail myself, but instead I'm thinking about you."

"That's a good place to start," he said.

Tory gave pause at the unexpected softness in his words. She was helpless when he spoke to her like that. When he was kind and gentle he was too perfect for words. She looked up at him. "I think it would be best if I got my own room."

"Best for whom?"

"For both of us."

"Don't speak for me, Tory. I'd like nothing more than to spend the night with you in my arms."

She glared at him. "There are two beds in here and don't be nice to me. You aren't making this any easier."

"Sorry." He crossed the room in a few strides and pulled her into the circle of his arms. Tory put a hand on his chest and found it as hard and unyielding as she'd imagined, her fingers curled into the soft cotton of his shirt.

"Sorry?"

He put a large hand up to her face, cupping her cheek and forcing her to look at him. "I'm not going to lie to you. I haven't been able to think of much of anything since I saw you in your bedroom that first night."

Protected in the circle of his arms, Tory closed her

eyes and allowed her cheek to rest against his chest. Would it be so awful to take what she wanted so much to give? She could forget about trials and criminals and money and dead people. Forget everything but the way he made her feel. She would keep this memory in her heart always.

His fingers danced over the outline of her spine, leaving a trail of electrifying sensation in their wake. Like a spring flower, passion flourished and blossomed from deep within her, filling her quickly with an unfamiliar type of frenzied desire. He ignited feelings so powerful and so intense that Tory felt panicky.

Panicky. Excited. Wanted. She slid her arms up his chest and wrapped them around his neck, standing on her toes to scatter kisses wherever she could reach. Her heart raced and her blood sang.

He touched her and she couldn't think anymore.

Clayton moved his hand in a series of slow, sensual circles until it rested against her rib cage, just under the swell of her breast. He wanted—no, needed to see her face. He wanted to see the desire in her eyes. Catching her chin between his thumb and forefinger, he tilted her head up with the intention of searching her eyes. He never made it that far.

His eyes were riveted to her lips, which were slightly parted, a glistening shade of pale rose. His eyes roamed over every delicate feature, and he could feel her heart rate increase through the thin fabric. A knot formed in his throat as he silently acknowledged his own incredible need for this woman.

Lowering his head, he was finally able to take that

first, tentative taste. Her mouth was warm and pliant, so was her body, which now pressed urgently against him. His hands roamed purposefully, memorizing every nuance and curve.

He felt his own body respond with an ache, then an almost overwhelming rush of desire surged through him. Her arms slid around his waist, pulling him closer. Clayton marveled at the perfect way they fit together. It was as if Tory had been made for him. For this.

"Tory," he whispered against her mouth. He toyed with a lock of her hair first, then slowly wound his hand through the silken mass and gave a gentle tug, forcing her head back even more. Looking down at her face, Clayton knew there was no other sight on earth as beautiful and inviting as her smoky hazel eyes.

In one effortless motion, he lifted her and carefully lowered her onto the bed, shoving folders onto the floor without caring. Her pale golden hair fanned out against the pillow.

She lifted her arms to him. "I think you're supposed to get on the bed with me," Tory said in a husky voice.

He braced one knee on the bed beside her hip. With a single finger, Clayton reached out to trace the delicate outline of her mouth. Her skin was smooth with a faint rosy flush. "Are you sure?" he asked in a tight voice, not sure how he would handle it if she uttered a rejection. He sucked in a breath and waited for her response.

"Very."

Sliding into place next to her, he began showering her face and neck with light kisses. While his mouth searched for that sensitive spot at the base of her throat, he felt her fingers working the buttons of his shirt.

He waited breathlessly for the feel of her hands on his body and he wasn't disappointed when the anticipation gave way to reality. A pleasurable moan spilled from his mouth when she brushed away his clothing and began running her palms over the taut muscles of his stomach.

Capturing both of her hands in one of his, Clayton gently held them above her head. The position arched her back, drawing his eyes down to the outline of her erect nipples.

"This isn't fair," she said as he slowly undid the buttons of her sweater.

"Believe me, Tory. If I let you keep touching me, I'd probably last less than a minute." He reassured her with a smile and a kiss.

Tory responded by lifting her body to him. The rounded swell of one exposed breast brushed his arm. He began peeling away her layers of clothing. He was rewarded by the incredible sight of her breasts spilling over the edges of a lacy undergarment. His eyes burned as he drank in the sight of the taut peaks straining against the lace. His hand rested first against the flatness of her stomach before inching up over the warm flesh. Finally his fingers closed over the rounded fullness.

"Please let me touch you!" Tory cried out.

"Not yet," he whispered as his thumb and forefinger released the front clasp on her bra. He ignored her futile struggle to release her hands as he dipped his head to kiss the raging pulse point at her throat. Her soft skin grew hot as he worked his mouth lower and lower. She gasped when his mouth closed around her nipple, then called his name in a hoarse voice that caused a tremor to run the full length of his body.

Moments later he lifted his head only long enough to see her passion-laden expression and to tell her she was beautiful.

"So are you."

Whether it was the sound of her voice or possibly the way she pressed herself against him, Clayton didn't know or care. He found himself nearly undone by the level of passion communicated by the movements of her supple body.

He reached down until his fingers made contact with a wisp of silk and lace. The feel of the sensuous garment against his skin very nearly pushed him over the edge. With her help, he was able to whisk the panties over her hips and legs, until she was finally next to him without a single barrier.

He sought her mouth again as he released his hold on her hands. He didn't know which was more potent, the feel of her naked body against his or the frantic way she worked to remove his clothing. His body moved to cover hers; his tongue thrust deeply into the warm recesses of her mouth. His hand moved downward, skimming the side of her body all the way to her thigh. Then, giving in to the urgent need pulsating through him, Clayton positioned himself between her legs. Every muscle in his body tensed as he looked at her face before directing his attention lower to the point where they would join. Tory lifted her hips, welcoming, inviting, as her palms flattened against his hips and tugged him toward her.

"I wish it could be this way forever," he groaned against her lips.

"Don't think about forever," she whispered back. "Not now. Just make love to me, please?"

He wasted no time responding to her request. In a single motion, he thrust deeply inside of her, knowing without question that he had found heaven on earth.

He wanted to treat her to a slow, building climax but with the feelings sweeping through him, it wasn't an option. He caught his breath and held it. The sheer pleasure of being inside of her sweet softness was just too powerful. She wrapped her legs around his hips just as the first explosive waves surged from him. One after the other, ripples of pleasure poured from him into her. Satisfaction had never been so sweet.

With his head buried next to hers, the sweet scent of her hair filled his nostrils. Clayton reluctantly relinquished possession of her body. It took several minutes before his breathing slowed to a steady, satiated pace. "I'm sorry," he began.

"Wh-why? I thought it went very...well."

Turning and bracing himself on his elbow, he peered down at her face. He couldn't help but smile. "It went well?" he parroted, watching her mouth pull into an annoyed line. Brushing her hair from her face, he planted a tender kiss on her flushed cheek. "I was very...selfish."

"It was really very—"

Placing his finger against her pretty lips, he quieted her, then traced the perfect shape of her mouth. "One-sided," he finished. "In my defense, you are very sexy, and it had been a long time. So, lie back, relax, and this time I'll get it right."

"Relax? Are you kidding? And what was wrong with what just happened?"

He laughed at her honesty. "If you'll be quiet for a few minutes, I'll show you."

A few minutes turned into several long, wonderful hours.

After righting the sheets to some degree, Tory curled into the welcoming strength of his big body. She heard and felt the strong, even rhythm of his heart. Draping her leg over his, she sighed loudly. "I now understand why they write songs and poems extolling the joys of carnal pleasures. My horizons are expanded. My understanding of the mysteries of life has blossomed. And I feel good." She delivered the last in a poor rendition of the James Brown classic.

He laughed, causing the hair on his chest to tickle her cheek. "You are wonderful for my ego. When I'm old and gray and I look back on tonight, I know I will remember this moment fondly."

"Think you'll be able to remember it?"

"Yes," he answered, his tone devoid of its earlier humor. "But not for the reason you think."

Chapter Fifteen

Not for the reason you think? Like thinking had any role whatsoever in her actions. And replaying it won't change anything, she reminded herself for the hundredth time in less than ten hours.

Over, done, finished.

She'd had sex with a man who didn't love her. Not part of her plan, yet well short of detonating a nuclear device.

No, the best plan—the safest plan—was to pretend it hadn't happened. Go on about her business as if nothing had changed. Because truth be told…it hadn't. Clayton had more important things to think about than her emotional needs. He was fighting for his freedom. If he failed, he'd spend the rest of his life in prison.

Compared to the gravity of that reality, her regrets over their casual transgression shouldn't matter. No. The very last thing he needed was her getting all clingy and insecure. She knew from the start that this was a temporary situation. Now it was time to buck up and act like an adult. He deserved that.

He's had enough pain and anguish. If she cared—and

she did—she'd put aside her own budding feelings and do the right thing. Clear his name, get a divorce, then walk away.

Her heart fell into the pit of her stomach. She tasted bitter disappointment. But it was tempered by the memory of being with him. Their time together would end but she'd have the memory of those hours for always.

Fluffing her freshly washed hair, she acknowledged she'd been hiding in the bathroom long enough. Pasting a bright smile in place, she took a fortifying breath and rejoined him.

Clayton greeted her with an intimate smile that sent a shiver dancing happily along her spine. Since he had yet to don a shirt, the shiver went to other parts of her body, as well. She swallowed.

"Need anything ironed while I'm at it?" he asked, putting the final press on his denim shirt.

"You iron. How enlightened of you."

His chuckle was deep and warm. "And they say prison can't change a man. I wonder if there will come a time when I'll fully appreciate my ironing skills. I also mastered peeling potatoes without shredding my knuckles."

"That's a marketable ability," she returned. Especially if he ironed shirtless in a storefront window. He could put out a tip jar, so legions of women could show their appreciation.

And she'd be first in line. An unobstructed view of those broad shoulders, muscled chest and arms, and that rock-hard stomach was well worth a hefty gratuity. His perfectly sculpted physique teamed with classic, dark features was a lethal combination. And she knew firsthand how very expertly he used his assets. He was a walking, talking pleasure machine, renewing the strong desire racing on her uneven pulse.

Strength. I need strength.

As if hearing her silent plea, Clayton shrugged into the shirt, buttoned it and then stuffed it inside the waistband of his khaki slacks. His ensemble, chosen quickly and charged to Pam's account, was casual, but there was something about the way he carried himself that gave the outfit class. Money and breeding always showed, she decided as she slipped into her black leather flats.

After devoting way too much time to their sex life—limited through it was—Tory turned her attention to their investigation.

"We need more information," she told him. "Someone who can tell us about those undetermined deaths."

Clayton grinned his agreement. "Meet Dr. Scott Edwards." He reached down, then passed her the duty roster she had printed the day before.

Scanning the pages, Tory counted the small hatch marks Clayton had placed next to the doctor's name. "He stopped seeing patients at Cresthaven a week after the last patient died."

Clayton had a hopeful gleam in his dark eyes. "He's listed as the primary physician in all the files."

"He could be involved," Tory cautioned. "He could even be Pam's partner."

"True. But we won't know until we go see him."

"You found him?"

Clayton nodded. "Got his number from Directory Assistance. You've got an appointment in an hour."

"Just me?"

He came and placed one hand against her cheek. Tory cringed, fearful that she'd melt and beg him to make love to her again. One time was understandable, letting it happen again would be stupid. She brushed his hand away and averted her eyes. Hearing his small intake of breath didn't help. She had no desire to hurt him, but it was time to practice preservation of self-interest.

"What's wrong?" he asked, his voice laced with concern.

"N-nothing." Tory set about gathering her purse.

She stilled when she felt Clayton's hand close on her shoulder. "Hey, what gives?"

Now for the awkward dissecting of the night before, she thought, flinching. If this had to happen, it was going to happen without him touching her. Using only her thumb and forefinger, she removed his hand as if it was some sort of insect.

Squaring her shoulders and concentrating to make her expression as bland as possible, she met his inquisitive dark eyes. "While I'd be a liar if I said I was sorry last night happened, I don't want it to happen again."

The proclamation registered in the slight clench of his jaw. Deep lines furrowed his brow. "It wasn't my idea."

She winced, knowing full well he was right. "I take full responsibility. I thought I could handle it, but, truth be told, sex without an emotional connection isn't for me." She paused and chose her next words carefully.

"The only thing we'll ever really share is a sordid history and a crime spree."

"I never pretended I could offer you happily ever after."

Knowing that and hearing it were different animals. It felt as if someone was tearing her heart into pieces, bit by agonizing bit. "I never expected you to," she acknowledged. While she appreciated his directness, she wasn't in any huge hurry to hear him share any more of it. "While I genuinely care about helping you clear your name and, by association, mine, I'd be the first one to stand up and shout that there is no future in this. That being the case, there also won't be any more sex in this."

"Fine by me," he returned easily.

Too easily. But this wasn't the time or place to contemplate the utter foolishness of allowing herself to fall in love with an escaped convict who just happened to be her husband.

She had grown comfortable with thinking of him as her husband. Acknowledging that she'd fallen for him was a startling revelation. Luckily, she'd kept it to herself. And it would stay that way.

If he could be casual, so could she. She'd be better than casual. Slapping her cheeriest expression in place, she asked, "So, where is this doctor?"

Dallas morning traffic reminded her of Baltimore. Too many cars, not enough lanes and lots and lots of horns and hand gestures.

Clayton got a little lost but managed to find the small medical complex in the shadow of the downtown glass-

and-steel skyscrapers built by the oil boom in the early eighties.

Dr. Edwards was a sole practitioner according to the sign affixed to the bland rectangular building that formed the base of the U-shaped trio of offices.

Tory was welcomed by a receptionist who handed her a clipboard with several forms. "I'll need to copy your insurance card."

She was about to reach for her wallet, when Clayton spoke up, "We're private pay."

The receptionist's brilliant fuchsia lips pursed, and her heavily lined eyes narrowed as she regarded them for a long, accusatory moment. "Payment is due in full before you can see the doctor. You understand."

"I'm not here for an exam, just a consultation," Tory replied, hoping excessive pleasantness would disarm the older woman's callous demeanor.

"And this isn't a free clinic. Either pay up-front or you don't get in to see the doctor. So, will it be cash, check or charge?"

"Charge," Tory practically purred as she slipped Pam's credit card across the laminate counter. She was only sorry that she wouldn't be around when the receptionist found out the card and the account were bogus.

The waiting room was decorated in a Western theme. Lots of rustic carvings, saloon prints and heavy leather furniture with brass rivets. The magazine selection was dated and varied. She could pass the time with everything from fishing tips to catching up on the latest happenings in the land of soap operas.

Clayton opted for a dated financial magazine while

ory reviewed the files they had brought along. They
ad been waiting for fifteen minutes when an older man
mbled through the door.

The nasty receptionist greeted him by name and let
im right back through the door marked Private. Tory
lanced at the clock, watching as another ten minutes
cked off slowly.

Finally they were shown into the back, down a short
all with six examination rooms. Piped music and the
trong scent of antiseptic filled the air. The small room
eld an exam table, a built-in shelf that probably dou-
led as a writing desk, a rolling stool and one metal
hair. The walls were cluttered with official memos
rom various health organizations and a full-size poster
f the gastrointestinal tract.

Clayton remained standing, offering her the chair.
While she sat down, he picked up a plastic model of the
eart and began taking it apart.

Keeping the files in a neat stack in her lap, Tory's
nood vacillated between anxiety and annoyance. She
new she had to keep both of those emotions in check.
hey needed Dr. Edwards's cooperation.

She was a little startled when he came into the
oom. She'd envisioned an older man, shock of white
air, maybe thick, framed glasses. Instead this man
vas tall, athletic, and looked to be in his early thir-
es. His dark blond hair was stylishly cut, just a frac-
on too long to be conservative. He had a ready smile
nd extended his hand even before the door had
losed.

"Good morning." He carried a small, empty folder

with Tory's name typed on a tab. "I'm Scott Edwards, what can I do for you today?"

Clayton shook the man's hand and answered, "We need some information."

"Please," the doctor said, indicating that Clayton should take the stool as he jumped up onto the exam table. The paper covering crinkled loudly. "I'll see what I can do. What body part is bothering you?" he asked with a grin.

"We aren't sick," Tory replied. "We're here about some of your patients from Cresthaven."

The doctor's expression slammed closed, and his whole demeanor changed. He was stiff and began nervously clicking the top of the pen in his hand. "I'm no longer affiliated with Cresthaven."

"That's what we want to talk about," Clayton explained.

"Who are you?" he asked.

Escaped prisoner, fleeing felons, murder suspects— take your pick, Tory thought.

"I'm a lawyer," she heard Clayton answer.

Safe, almost true.

"Who's your client?" Edwards inquired. "Never mind. We can stop here. I've got my own lawyer. You should really speak to him regarding any litigation you're contemplating."

The doctor started to leave, but Clayton's next comment stopped him. "I don't want to sue you. I want to help you."

Edwards looked at them with suspicion narrowing his blue eyes. "Why am I having a hard time believing that?"

"It's true," Tory insisted, thrusting the files in front of him.

Edwards scanned the collection of records and lifted
is head. If she had any doubt that something wasn't
ght, it was confirmed instantly.

"Where did you get these?" he asked.

Clayton sat down on the stool and rolled it over next
the doctor. Ignoring the question, he said, "You were
e primary physician but you didn't certify these deaths
natural. Why?"

"That's confidential."

Clayton shook his head. "Death certificates are
ublic records, doctor-patient confidentiality doesn't
ontrol."

Rubbing his face, the doctor seemed to wage an in-
rnal struggle before finally speaking. "These patients
ere gravely ill."

"But?" Tory prompted.

He shrugged. "Their deaths weren't unexpected, just
dden. Normally you'd see a decline before a patient
xpires. Not necessarily a long one, especially if the pa-
ent in question is quite old. I was there every day. I saw
ese people every day. I didn't see anything to indicate
eath was imminent. None of the nurses did, either."

"So, what are you saying?"

"Nothing," he answered quickly, then amended his
ne. "I'm not sure. The medical examiner's office refused
do even brief physical exams. Not a top priority when
person over eighty dies quietly in a nursing home."

"What do you think happened?"

"I'm not sure anything *did* happen," he insisted. "I
st wasn't comfortable with so many sudden deaths. But
never found anything to link the deaths, and the board

insisted I drop it. I threatened to leave if they didn't in
vestigate. I thought that would light a fire under them.

"It didn't?"

He shook his head. "Hardly. Cresthaven caters to
very wealthy clientele. The fear of losing some of the
wealthy residents was a greater concern than a rook
doctor's unproven theories."

"Any guesses?" Clayton queried. "Anyone yo
thought might be suspicious?"

"All of the employees are thoroughly screened an
most of them have been there for years," Doctor Ed
wards explained.

"What about visitors?" Tory asked.

Again, Edwards shrugged. "Nothing out of the ord
nary. Relatives came and went."

Remembering Frankie's line of work, Tory aske
"What about deliveries? Were there any new deliver
people?"

"I wasn't there 24/7," he replied. "Mrs. Banks woul
know. She's the purchasing agent for Cresthaven. Bee
doing it for decades."

"Do you think she'd give you a list of deliveries?
Clayton asked.

He nodded. "Probably. I can give her a call."

"Would you?" Tory felt a surge of renewed enthusiasm

"Now?" the doctor asked. He agreed and excuse
himself. Twenty minutes later he returned carrying se
eral sheets of paper. "This is a list of delivery dates an
the corresponding companies for the past five years."

"Thanks," she heard Clayton say as he shared a han
shake with the young doctor.

"If you find anything," Edwards began, "let me know. It could be coincidence, but I'd like to know either way."

"You got it."

Clayton drove to the closest restaurant and parked. After escorting Tory to one of the booths, he slipped into place and set the papers on the table.

He was oblivious to his surroundings. Well, almost oblivious. The effect of having Tory so close was never too far removed from his consciousness. He didn't need to look up to know that she'd clipped her hair up, leaving just a few wispy strands around her face and against her long, elegant neck. He knew her shirt had a funky print and left about an inch of skin exposed before tight-fitting jeans hugged her slender hips. Her legs were long and shapely, not muscular but toned. Most of all he knew that beneath the clothing was an incredibly hot body. An off-limits hot body.

He felt himself frown but masked it by sipping the coffee just delivered to their table. Though he had thoroughly enjoyed their encounter, he reluctantly acknowledged her assessment at been right on. He had nothing to offer her. His life was a tornado—spinning turmoil with no predictable direction and the ability to destroy everything in its path.

He could go back to prison. And even if he cleared his name, he was back at square one. No life, no career. None of the things he felt sure were important to a woman like Tory.

"Twenty-four hours," Tory excitedly gushed, waving a sheet of paper in his direction. Her eyes shone with promise and her face positively glowed. "A truck from Frankie's warehouse made a delivery to Cresthaven within twenty-four hours of each questionable death."

Revived by this positive turn, Clayton took the paper from her. For an instant his fingers brushed hers, and he felt a bolt of energy flash at the point of contact. It took specific effort to keep from being sidetracked by his attraction to her.

"So somehow Frankie sent a flunky to Texas, who did something that caused a resident to die. Then Frankie contacts Pam?"

Tory was quiet for a moment. "We're still missing something. Like, how were the people killed? And who selected the victims?"

"My guess is Frankie."

"My guess is Pam," Tory countered.

"Why?"

"Because it was all about stealing their assets, and Pam was all about money."

"So where to now?"

"Newspaper archives," she supplied. "We need to know more about the victims."

"YOU'RE REALLY BAD at this," Tory chided in a stern whisper.

Clayton cast her a look. "I didn't need to learn research skills. In my former life, I had you to do that for me."

"Watch and learn," she instructed, wiggling into the seat in front of the computer terminal they shared.

He was watching. And learning. He learned that when concentrating, she drew her lower lip between her teeth. He learned her hair had highlights that shimmered in the sunlight streaming through the lone window of the library's reference room. He knew she typed with her pinkies in the air and her nails were polished a pale shade of peach that set off her exotic skin.

"You're supposed to be looking at the screen, not me." She spoke without ever diverting her attention from the task.

"You're much more attractive than a computer." He caught one of the loose tendrils of hair at the side of her graceful neck and rubbed its silken texture.

"Focus, Clayton," she warned.

"Oh, I'm focused," he insisted, abandoning the hair in favor of trailing his forefinger along the graceful edge of her jawline.

"We're supposed to be learning about the dead people."

"Mmm-hmm," he leaned over to deliver his answer against her ear.

"Clayton?" There was a slight catch in the breathy way she'd said his name.

He liked that. Yeah, yeah, he knew it would be better for them both in the long run if he kept his distance and didn't complicate an already bizarre situation. That was all well and good in theory. But she wasn't a theory. She was a living, breathing woman that needed only to be within touching distance for all his well-intended convictions to evaporate.

"I'll leave you to navigate the newspaper archives all alone if you don't keep your hands to yourself."

"We could go up in the stacks and fool around," he suggested as his lips brushed her soft, warm flesh. "The archives will still be here when we get back. That's why they're called archives."

She shoved him gently. "Behave. Last warning or I'm outta here."

Grudgingly he moved away from her, enjoying the lingering taste of her on his lips. He felt as if he'd had a small sip of fabulous wine. Only it wasn't enough. He wanted the whole bottle.

"Okay, I've found some stuff about the first one. Mrs. Sylvia Carson-Cavanaugh. Died nearly five years ago," she read. "Philanthropist, active in her church, involved alumna at Hawthorne College, now Hawthorne University, in Dallas. Past president of the City Garden Club. Past pres—"

"Hawthorne?" Clayton repeated.

She turned and met his eyes. "Is that important?"

"Pam went to Hawthorne."

Chapter Sixteen

Hawthorne University was a massive complex situated about seven miles east of the city. According to the signs posted just before the arching oaks overhanging the main drive, it had served the educational and community needs since its founding in 1888.

Like so many old colleges, the buildings were stately, domed and named after prominent people in the development and cultural history of the state.

Clayton had been there two other times, both with Pam. Their first trip was prior to their marriage and he didn't really recall the details. The second visit had been about six months after the wedding, when Pam had convinced him to make a hefty donation so her name would appear prominently among alumni patrons.

Now, in early September, the place was filled with students. Some hurried, others lounged on the grassy knolls around the quad, still more gathered in various-size groups. He could hear muffled conversations, music, laughter as he parked and led Tory toward the main library. The odor of freshly mowed grass competed with the greasy smell of fried food.

Taking the marble steps two at a time, he reached the impressive door and yanked on the polished brass handle. He let Tory in first, then followed her into the brightly lit building.

Though the exterior was Victorian, the interior had been renovated into a large, open floor plan with four stories of glassed-in walkways and miles of computer cables. It looked more like flight control than a library.

After consulting the directory, they went to the third floor and found the collection of yearbooks.

Tory read off the names, while Clayton thumbed through the dusty books. His first hunch had been wrong. "She didn't belong to the same sorority as Pam. Majored in home sciences." He paused and grinned at Tory. "And she was the recording secretary for the sewing club her junior year."

"That was worth the tuition," Tory responded dryly. "She probably wasn't allowed in a lot of the serious clubs back then. She was forging the way for women of my generation to fully participate in the educational experience."

"True, but it doesn't get us any closer to understanding why or how she was selected by Pam and her accomplices."

Reshelving that volume, Clayton set about finding the next alumnus. He repeated the process for all of the victims and wasn't any closer to finding a link.

Tory read the annoyance in his drawn face and went to him. Resting her head against his chest, she flattened her palm against the solid muscles. Giving a reassuring pat with one hand, she then looped her arm around his waist and offered an encouraging hug. Drinking in the clean scent of him, she wished more than anything that she could blink her eyes and miraculously conjure the answer to this puzzle.

"You know," she began, moving and pulling him along by his belt loop, "we need to regroup." She found a quiet table against the back wall of the library.

She started to sit, but Clayton wrapped her in his arms and held her close. He pressed a shower of small kisses on top of her head. It felt nice. Safe.

Dangerous.

"Sit," she commanded, not trusting the last shred of willpower that kept her from bending him over the table and kissing him senseless. "Let's review."

"You have beautiful breasts."

Her cheeks burned and she narrowed her eyes to offer a reproachful glare. "Let's review *relevant* facts about everything that's happened thus far."

Shrugging, Clayton laced his fingers and scooted his chair closer to the table. "I broke out of jail. I married you. I—"

"From the beginning," she corrected. "You and Pam had a fight."

"Pam's instigation, not mine," he insisted. "One of her neighbors called 911 after hearing screams. The cops found blood all over the place. I was arrested, tried and convicted. I escaped and here we are."

Tilting her head, she smiled at his brief synopsis. "Pam started the fight that day?"

"She was itching for it," Clayton assured her with a scowl. "I never understood why she was so furious about the divorce. We hadn't been in love for a long time."

"So she picked a fight, then coincidentally went back home and was killed?" Tory asked, still puzzled by that aspect of the fact pattern.

"They didn't find her body, but yes. They found a lot of blood, and even though there was a lab screwup that made it impossible to do more than test for type, there was enough for two doctors to swear a person couldn't lose that much blood at one time and survive. Now I'm betting her accomplice must have killed her. Maybe he knew about the fight we'd had and just took advantage of the opportunity."

That was one possibility, Tory acknowledged. "So Pam and her accomplices were killing defenseless, old, rich people who went to college here. Pam was the banker. Her accomplice killed her before he knew where she'd stashed the money? That doesn't make sense."

Clayton sighed. "Criminals aren't always the brightest beers in the six-pack. Maybe Pam and her accomplice struggled and her murder was accidental."

"Then why kill Frankie Hilton?" Tory countered.

"To keep him from exposing the murders."

"But no one has ever called them murders. So Pam's murder was about Pam." She went over to the shelving, ran her fingers along the bindings and pulled the leather book from its place.

In the index she found three listings under Pam's name. The first was a standard head shot. The second was a photograph of Pam taken during a sorority-sponsored blood drive. Scrutinizing the picture, Tory could find nothing out of the ordinary. The final picture had been taken at a dance. It showed the half-dozen young women in formal gowns wearing the sashes and crowns of the Greek system royalty.

"Did Pam keep in contact with anyone in particular?" she asked, disappointed that nothing leaped off the page at her.

"A few of her sorority sisters."

"What about men from the campus?" Tory asked.

"Yeah, a guy named Abrams, David. Donald. Darren. Something with a *D*," Clayton answered after a brief pause. "They met here and then went on to law school in Montana together. I only met him a couple of times. Washed out of law school and switched to an MBA. Ended up as some sort of auditor in Helena. I think he had a thing for Pam."

"Let's look him up." Tory found Davis Abrams. He was an attractive guy and oddly similar to Clayton. Dark hair, intense eyes, not as handsome, but then few men were.

Aside from the mandatory head shot, Davis's only other mention was a group photo of him and the brothers from his fraternity. Tory experienced a real thrill of excitement as her eyes scanned the page. "Look at this!" She spun the book and passed it to him. "Look at the picture!"

"Is this him?" Clayton asked, tapping one of the small, dark heads almost too fuzzy to make out.

"Not the photograph, look at the photo credit."

"Photograph courtesy of Harry Greer Studios," Clayton read, his eyes widening.

"Wanna bet he's related to the Michael Greer who attacked you in prison?"

"We're going to find out," Clayton promised, and then he swooped her up into his strong arms.

He smothered her with loud, purposeful kisses as he spun her around in the small space. Tory giggled like a child, drawing the attention of several spectators.

It wasn't until they were shushed by five people that Tory's feet again touched the ground. She was giddy and dizzy and felt a real sense of hope for the first time since this whole escapade had begun.

But her joy was tempered by the very real fact that Clayton's wrongful incarceration wasn't the only thing coming to an end.

"THIS IS PRETTY FANCY," Tory commented as they approached the small gallery.

He had to agree. Harry Greer was obviously a pretty successful guy. They entered the Fort Worth establishment, and a bell above the door rang. In no time a slight man in a conservative dark suit appeared from the back. He smiled beneath the pencil-thin mustache that Clayton thought made it look like his lip had an eyebrow.

"Welcome," he said in a cultured Southern drawl. "What may I show you this afternoon?"

"Harry Greer prints?" Clayton asked.

The little man's lip curled unpleasantly, and one shaped brow drew up sharply. Theatrically he waved his arms as if presenting royalty and asked, "Have you looked around? We handle legitimate works of photographic art. If you are interested in second-rate snapshots, I suggest you go to your local mall."

"This was the last address we could find for Harry Greer," Tory explained.

"Well, your sources are quite out-of-date. I bought

this space from Mr. Greer almost two years ago." The stuffy little man twirled on his heel.

"Wait!" Clayton called out, not willing to accept this setback without an argument. "It's really important that I find Mr. Greer. Do you have a forwarding address?"

"In the back," he answered with an annoyed sigh.

Clayton didn't really care how annoyed the guy was. He needed to find Harry Greer.

Tory studied some of the photographs while the snooty little guy was out of the room. She seemed to be enjoying them, but the stark black-and-white compositions were lost on Clayton. He didn't know much about art or photography, and standing in an empty room staring at desolate images didn't expand his knowledge base.

As promised the owner returned with a small card that he thrust at Clayton. "Mr. Greer is a…lesser talent. If you would like, I can show you some wonderful works that have both quality and aesthetic value."

He saw Tory offer a broad, stunning smile that seemed to take some of the starch out of the gallery owner's stiff demeanor. "That would be wonderful, but we're pressed for time right now."

"We could arrange an appointment."

"We'll get back to you," Clayton promised, hooking Tory's arm and leading her out of the shop.

"So it isn't your taste," she grumbled, yanking her arm free. "I liked some of the photographs."

"We're fugitives," he reminded her. "Not decorators."

"Right. So where to now?"

Clayton unfolded the page and stopped in midstride. At the same instant Tory's purse started playing the

"1812 Overture." Pulling the cell phone from her purse, she read the displayed information.

"It's my office," she said, then turned to discover Clayton had stopped several yards back.

Spinning, she jogged back to where he was planted on the sidewalk, holding the phone out as the digitized serenade continued. "It's my office!" she repeated, breathless. "Should I answer it?"

"Wh-what? No! Your position can be located by tri-angulating cell transmission towers."

"How do you know that?" she asked, impressed. "More prison trivia," she guessed.

"*Court TV,*" he countered with a broad grin. "Very popular viewing in the day room."

Using her fingernail, Tory switched the phone on to vibrate and slipped it back into her purse.

"Time for another road trip," Clayton announced.

"Where is Greer?"

"Montana."

Her heart sank. Several scenarios raced through her mind. None of them good. "We can't go back there!" she said flatly. "Not until we have hard proof of your innocence."

He peered down at her with an expression that was equal parts carefully guarded fear and honest appreciation. But she didn't want his gratitude. She wanted—no *needed* to know that he wouldn't end up back in prison.

"Unfortunately, I think the proof is in Montana," he explained gently. The pad of his thumb moved up to trace the fine lines around her mouth. "Greer is in Montana, and right now he's the only lead we've got."

"But the police!"

"I'll be careful," he insisted.

"We'll be careful," she corrected.

Clayton's eyes filled with emotion. "No, Tory, I think it's time for me to go it alone. I'll drop you someplace along the route and you—"

"Absolutely not. We started this together and we're finishing it together."

"I don't want to be responsible for you."

She bristled. "You aren't responsible for me. We're in this for better or worse, remember?"

His smile vanished and his face became a stony, unreadable mask. "I didn't mean those words when I said them. Getting you to marry me was a test. I still wasn't sure I could trust you. I half expected you to bail on the whole idea. And I never intended you to *want* to assume the role of my wife."

That was a hot poker to the soul! "I don't want that role," she shot back, stinging from his harsh words. The sham of pretending to be his wife for the sake of convenience held no appeal whatsoever. "I didn't ask for any of this. But since you dragged me into it and I'm now wanted by the police, I intend on sticking it out to the very end."

"It isn't your choice," he countered.

"I'm making it my choice."

"I don't want you to get arrested."

She made a derisive sound. "A little late for that, don't you think?"

"I simply meant I didn't want to watch when it happened."

"Neither do I," she replied, feeling some of the anger fade. "So we'll just have to plan very carefully and stay under the radar."

He placed his hands on her shoulders and held her gaze. "I want to know that you can walk away from this. I need to know that when this is over, you'll be able to go on with whatever life you want without ever looking back on the horrible memory of being in jail. I know what it's like and I don't want that for you."

"Don't worry about me. I'm tough, Clayton. I'll emerge from this just fine. I'll move someplace new. Eventually, I'm sure, I'll meet a decent guy. I'll have a family, and when I'm old and gray, I'll gather my grandchildren at my feet and regale them with tales of my days as a fugitive."

"That sounds good, but if we get caught, you can forget everything but the part about living someplace new. You'll be a guest of the state, and believe me, it isn't a great life."

She was angry. Really, really angry. Did he actually think she would quietly slink off with a "thanks, honey" and a pat on the head?

"It can't be too much worse than being forced into a marriage with you."

"You could have refused."

Looking directly into his eyes, she said, "I wish I had."

Chapter Seventeen

"I'm never taking another road trip as long as I live," Tory groaned when they arrived at a small motel about fifty miles east of Jasper. It seemed like a lifetime ago that they'd left Montana and now here they were. Back again.

"You've been on the news more, so you should stay out of sight," Tory said. "Wait here while I get a room."

After more than twenty-four hours in the car, she was fantasizing about a hot tub and the chance to lie flat on her back. Possibly all at once. Twisting her hair up and tucking it into a bun, she headed toward the office and said a silent prayer not to be recognized.

It was too easy. The woman behind the desk barely looked away from the television as she passed Tory all the paperwork to secure the room. As she had done before, Tory registered as Pam, then passed the credit card across the dusty ledge.

The establishment was pretty beaten down. The lobby—which wasn't really a lobby but rather a small square room dominated by a large cardboard cutout of a grizzly bear with an advertisement for hunting rifles—smelled of old coffee and stale tobacco. There were two chairs with tattered upholstery, arranged unevenly on a rug with more spots than a Dalmatian.

"Didn't clear."

"Wh-what?" Tory stammered.

"The credit card was rejected. Pay in cash or move along."

Thankfully, she had enough cash in her purse to cover the bill. She hurriedly handed it to the woman and was given a large gold-tone key attached to a plastic bob in exchange.

"Checkout is noon."

"Not a problem," Tory assured the woman.

"Gotta pay in full before then, if you plan on staying another night."

"Okay." She wanted to get out of there. Having the credit card rejected was embarrassing, but not nearly as problematic as being recognized. Key in hand, she quickly departed for the anonymity of her rented room.

Clayton joined her a few minutes later. He looked tired and haggard. The shadow of a beard had grown dark, and lack of sleep gave him a gaunt, slightly dangerous appearance. He barely managed to put their bags on the floor before falling face first on top of the bed.

It squeaked and buckled under his weight. There was a musty, dank smell in the air that was as depressing as the decor. The single bed was adorned by a faded tropical bedspread that looked completely out of place in a rustic Montana motel.

Rustic was too kind, she decided. The place was a dive, but it was a clean dive and her choices were limited.

"I think I'm permanently crippled," Clayton moaned against the mattress, then rolled onto his back.

Tory felt his eyes on her as she started putting together the things she needed for her bath. It wasn't the first time, either. She'd awakened from a fitful nap during their latest trip and found him glancing at her at regular intervals. It was disquieting, especially since she felt he owed her an apology for the argument.

"Do you want the shower first, or may I take it?"

A slow grin curved his lips. "We could go together, conserve water."

It was really hard to be mad at a guy who looked so positively wonderful. But she wanted to be mad. Mad was better than getting mired in self-pity. What had he said? He hadn't meant his wedding vows? Did she really believe that somewhere in the midst of the strange odyssey he'd have a lightbulb moment and decide he was madly in love with her?

You did, stupid, her brain taunted.

"It was a joke. No need to look so horrified," he remarked.

Tory shrugged. "I'm just exhausted."

"No, you're upset with me."

No, no and no. I don't want to fight. I'm too tired and too…in love with you! She glanced back, silently praying that he drop the subject. It didn't work.

"Do you always hold a grudge this long?"

"Nope, I pretty much decided you deserved special treatment. Really, Clayton, get off it."

"We could talk."

And hear you tell me how disposable I am in the

grand scheme of things? Pass, thanks. "We've covered all the important things," she insisted as she cradled her small collection of bath products.

"But I don't like the fact that you're annoyed at me."

"I'm not, not really," she admitted, especially to herself. "I'm annoyed at life in general. It's been a difficult few days."

His eyes roamed her face. "A long bath will improve your mood. I've noticed you're very fond of soaking in the tub."

"I'm a cheap date," she teased, grudgingly giving in to a timid smile. "Speaking of which, I think we maxed out Pam's credit card. We should switch to one of the others."

"How did we do that?" he asked.

"A shopping spree in Las Vegas. Hotels, motels, the rental car, cash advances, gas, restaurants."

"I get the picture. Go soak, I'll see if I can find someplace that will deliver food."

An hour later he was doing his best to arrange something that looked like a dinner table out of the lopsided bedside stand. What it lacked in ambiance it made up for in smell. The fried chicken and sides had his mouth watering and he was so hungry that he was ready to drag Tory out of the bathroom if need be.

His hand was on the knob with just that in mind when she emerged, squeezing water from her hair, wrapped in a towel that barely covered her from chest to thigh. His hunger demanded a completely new kind of satisfaction.

"If you walk around in a towel, there will be sex."

Tossing him a quick glance, she padded over and pulled some clothing out of the bag. She could have pulled an angry pit bull out of there and he wouldn't have noticed. All he saw was long, shapely legs, the teasing slope of her hips and a towel that she clutched precariously to her breasts.

"Dinner smells good. Be right out," she dashed back into the bath.

He wanted her. Badly. All he had to do was open the door and he was fairly certain that he could coax out her own needs, as well. If not, at least he'd have a great time trying.

Until reality set in. He sighed. Moving to where he'd arranged their meal, Clayton listened to the muffled sounds of Tory in the next room. The scent of her floral soap hung in the air. Every breath turned into a not-so-subtle reminder of her. Or, rather, a reminder of how he couldn't have her.

Pressing his fingertips into his temples, he struggled to refocus his thoughts. It didn't help.

There was only one bed. One small bed. To share. No touching. Nothing. How the hell was he going to manage that?

VERY BADLY, as it turned out. The next morning he felt worse than if he hadn't bothered trying to sleep at all. For a small woman, Tory sure could take up a lot of bed. She'd slept soundly. Arms and legs brushing against him until he was forced to lie rigidly on the small sliver she'd allotted him. Very rigidly. One part of his anatomy had been particularly rigid. Painfully so.

And it wasn't getting a whole lot better, he acknowledged when she returned to the room with a cardboard tray of coffee and sweet rolls. She was wearing the low-riding jeans, the ones that revealed teasing little peeks of flesh when she moved. He groaned.

"Hard night?"

He smiled dryly. "Very."

"Sorry. When the credit card was denied, I got so flustered I forgot to ask for two beds."

Dragging his eyes off the perfectly rounded navel in the center of her flawlessly flat tummy, Clayton reached for some coffee. "We need to take care of that today," he commented. "We're both low on cash, so we'll stop on our way up the west pass to where Greer lives."

After an infusion of caffeine, they loaded the car, not willing to risk staying in one place for too long. Soon they set off for the next destination. Clayton stuck to back roads and waited until they were in a busy shopping area before he stopped to replenish their finances.

He waited in the car while Tory went in. He was starting to be concerned when she didn't return after a few minutes. His apprehension increased as he watched each minute tick off on the dashboard clock. Scanning the parking area and the adjacent street, he felt some relief when he didn't see anything unusual. Cracking the window, he listened intently for the sound of sirens.

"And if the cops come?"

He didn't want to think about that. Nonetheless, his stomach churned at the thought. An image of Tory being thrown on the ground and cuffed brought the bitter taste of genuine fear to his tongue. Suddenly his mouth was dry.

Just as suddenly she came outside, hurrying toward the car. Concern marred her pretty features.

"They're all useless," she gushed on a breath as she got in the car.

"All of them?"

She nodded. "Drive. We'll go see Greer and then I'll figure something out."

"I thought you activated several of the accounts."

"I did. Maybe the police figured it out and they've frozen the accounts."

"I don't see how," Clayton countered. "There would be no reason for a—your purse is shaking."

"It's my phone," she explained. "It's on vibrate. My office keeps calling."

"Now that's probably the cops," Clayton told her. "I'm sure they're all over your office by now."

"The partners will love that," she drawled.

Clayton offered an apologetic glance before pointing the car in the direction of Greer's address. "Well, you said you wanted to leave Montana, anyway."

"Not as a disgrace," she joked, with a gloomy little laugh. "When I start looking for another job, I'll be a little light on references."

"You don't know that."

"Think about it, Clayton. My current employer will probably fire me. My previous employers are a murder victim and a convicted killer. Not exactly the kind of references that land the great jobs."

"If it's any consolation, my future prospects aren't so great, either."

"I...I'm sorry. You're right. Anything I might experience can't hold a candle to what you've gone through. And I know it won't be easy, but I'm sure you'll land on your feet."

"I'm a disbarred lawyer," he stated, hating the way it sounded.

"Your license to practice will be reinstated once you clear your name."

"Let's hope. I've never wanted to do anything but practice law."

"So you will."

She sounded so sure that Clayton found it infectious. He had a glimmer of hope and Tory to thank for that. He would clear his name, go back to work and…

And what? his brain challenged. The burning question.

The road leading to Greer's place was a winding dirt road with strange ropes strung on either side. Every few feet a metal pole lurched out of the ground to tether the rope in place. Odd. Something she'd never seen before. It wasn't substantial enough to be a fence. But there it was, nylon climbing rope that stretched from the highway up to the small cabin nestled in the trees.

The house was modest but normal enough. Though plain. No landscaping. No pots, plants or porch furniture. Had it not been for the curl of dark smoke rising from the stone chimney, she might have assumed the place was deserted.

"There's no car and no garage," she whispered as they approached the door.

Finding no bell, Clayton pounded against the solid door, then they waited.

As was the case every time they encountered a new

face, Tory was terrified of being recognized. Every muscle in her body tensed as she waited for the door to open.

The minute it did, she realized her fears were pointless.

He was average height, dressed in a plaid flannel shirt and pants that seemed a size too big. She hadn't expected such a young man. Harry couldn't have been much more than thirty-five. He didn't look like an aspiring photographer. It wasn't the disheveled clothes or the plain surroundings. It was the large, black glasses covering his eyes.

"Yes?"

"Mr. Greer? Mr. Harry Greer?"

"Uh-huh," he grunted, his head tilting to one side. "Who are you?"

"I'm with the department of corrections," she heard Clayton lie. Well, technically, it wasn't a lie, just a liberal use of the truth. "My name is Burns, Robert Burns." Clayton reached down and clasped the man's withered hand. "This is my assistant, Georgia Chain."

"Are you here about Mikey?" he asked, his tone harsh. "I've already given my statement to the cop who was here."

"May we come in?" Tory asked.

Reluctantly, Harry led the way. He moved through the house by skimming his fingers against furniture. The place could use a good cleaning, but he seemed to get along well enough.

It wasn't until Tory spied hundreds of framed and matted prints stacked against the far wall that she felt the first pangs of sympathy for the poor guy. As Clayton sat in the living room, Tory went over and started going through the images. They dated back for years and some were actually quite good. Much different from the college shots, these were decent compositions of appealing subjects. Judging by the content, she guessed most were taken in Texas.

"I was getting pretty good," Harry said, though he sat still. "Until my accident."

"These are lovely," Tory said. "I particularly like the candid shots. Where did you take them?"

"In and around Dallas," he answered. "Course, that was before my accident. Mixed the wrong chemicals and poof, no eyesight."

"Sorry," they muttered in unison.

"Can't change what is," Harry sighed heavily. "Mikey convinced me to come out here to live a few years back. He thought being around old friends would be good for me."

"Old friends?" Clayton prompted.

"My college roommate lives out here. Even though I dropped out after two years, he and I stay in touch. He even got my kid brother a job, and then Mikey went and got into trouble. Then…well, you know. Dave's been really good to me since Mikey died."

"Dave?" Clayton queried.

"Dave Abrams. He works down in Helena, but he comes up here when he can. Keeps me in groceries."

"Davis Abrams?" Tory asked.

Harry smiled. "Yep. Helluva decent guy. You know him?"

"We've met," Clayton answered. "He works for the state, right?"

"That's him. Pencil pusher. So, Mr. Burns, what is it I can do for you?"

"We just wanted to check in on you, see how you were getting along," Clayton answered, then he mouthed, "Let's get out of here," at Tory.

"I appreciate it, but I'm still thinking of suing. My brother had his faults, but he didn't deserve to die in prison."

"Well, good luck with that," Clayton managed.

Tory swatted his arm, it wasn't like Harry Greer was responsible for his younger brother's sins.

"So," Tory asked as they climbed back into the car and made a U-turn down the dirt road, "is Davis Abrams the brains behind all this? Where did you get that name, Mr. Burns, anyway?"

Clayton smiled as he started the engine. He gave her a little wink then said, "Robert E. Burns was an author. His novel was turned into an Academy-Award-winning film about prison reform."

Tory racked her brain for a minute. Robert Burns. *Georgia Chain.* "Fugitive from a Georgia Chain Gang?"

"It seemed appropriate," Clayton acknowledged. "And back to your question, I'm having a hard time picturing Davis Abrams as some brilliant criminal mastermind."

"Why?"

"He seemed pretty harmless. And I definitely can't see him killing Pam. Accidentally or otherwise, it wouldn't happen. Davis was in love with Pam."

"If he loved her, then maybe his passions got away from him."

Clayton laughed. "Wait until you meet him. I don't think Davis has passions."

After checking the gas gauge, Tory reminded him that they needed to address their financial issues. "There's an office place," she suggested, pointing to a small shop in a strip mall advertising computer access.

The shop was small, only three computer terminals available for rent. After filling out the forms and giving a cash deposit, she took Clayton over to the terminal and got to work.

Using the information printed on the credit card, she accessed the secure server and attempted to view the account with the PIN number she had arranged earlier.

Access denied.

She tried again. Same result.

"May I use the phone? It's toll free," she explained to the counter attendant. "Thanks," she said as she returned to the terminal.

"What's the problem?" Clayton asked in a whisper.

"We're about to find out." She navigated through the firewall of automation until she got a living breathing human on the line.

"I'm having trouble accessing my account," Tory explained.

"One moment." The sound of computer keys tapping came over the line. "Password change. Per your request, Mrs. Landry."

Tory held the phone at an angle so Clayton could also hear the customer service representative.

"How do I unchange my mind?" she asked.

"I can do that for you. First you'll have to answer a few security questions."

"O-okay."

"Date of birth?"

Clayton flashed the answer with his fingers.

"Seven, nine, seventy-two."

"Mother's maiden name?"

Again, Clayton provided the correct answer.

"Pet's name?"

Tory looked up and saw Clayton struggling for the answer. Finally, he mouthed a name. "Bitsy."

"Thank you, Mrs. Landry. Remote access to your account has been restored. Is there anything else we can do for you?"

"Thanks, no."

She placed the phone on the cubicle next to her and went back to the computer. True to her word, the customer service representative had solved the problem.

"Oh, my!" she exclaimed.

"Maxed out?" Clayton asked.

"I don't think that is possible," she said, swallowing her amazement. "I found…I found—"

"What?" he demanded.

"The money, Clayton," she blurted out in an excited whisper. "Pam put the money from the scam against her cards. These four accounts have credit balances of more than half a million dollars."

"Are you sure?"

She nodded enthusiastically, pulling the other cards out of her wallet to perform the same steps. An hour later they had found more than 1.3 million dollars.

"Amazing," Clayton breathed once they returned to the car. "All that money was right there all this time and no one knew."

"It's a smart system," Tory agreed. "Huge bank transactions cause red flags, but who thinks to check credit cards for overpayments?"

"My dear departed ex-wife," Clayton grunted. "No wonder Michael Greer was willing to kill me to find it. That's a lot of ready cash." Clayton drove back toward their motel.

"I feel sorry for his brother," Tory commented. "I think— This can't be good."

Two hundred yards ahead, a line of police cars had created a roadblock.

"How did they know we were in the area?"

"Who knows," he responded, distracted as he made a sudden turn and drove the rental off the main highway.

She watched as his eyes darted from the road, to the mirrors, then repeated the cycle. His knuckles were white where he gripped the steering wheel. The two-lane road didn't offer much in the way of protection. It was a flat, open highway that left them totally exposed should a helicopter appear overhead.

"What are we going to do?" she asked, swallowing the panic threatening to choke her.

"I'm working on a plan," Clayton said.

Though she appreciated the sentiment and the calm tone of his voice, she struggled to keep from completely losing it. At any second, she half expected to have a small army of law enforcement bear down on them, guns blazing.

Clayton surprised her when he pulled the car off onto the side of the road and killed the engine.

"Why are we stopping?"

"You've got to buy me some time."

"Okay," she agreed, not following at all.

"You've got to go to the cops."

"They'll arrest me!"

"Probably," he agreed apologetically.

"How does that help you?"

"Just tell them I've been holding you hostage. Tell them I stole the gun from your apartment and shot Frankie in Las Vegas. Tell them I've been driving you all over the country and that you finally managed to escape and went right to them."

"It won't work. Too many people have seen us together. They'll never buy that I wasn't complicit."

"It's our best option," Clayton argued. "While the cops are sorting out your sudden appearance, I can track down Davis."

She gripped his arm, allowing her fingers to dig into the flesh. "Let the authorities handle it, Clayton. We've got almost enough to clear you."

"Almost lands me back in jail," he insisted. "Give me something to write on."

"Why?"

"Just do it," he fairly growled.

Quickly he scribbled something then thrust the paper into her purse.

"Give me your wedding ring," he said.

She complied, twisting it from her finger and putting it into his open palm.

"Don't mention the wedding. We can sort that ou when I resurface."

Grabbing her by the back of the neck, Clayto crushed his mouth to hers. The kiss was deep and i tense, almost desperate, and it left her brain spinning

He started to get out of the car.

"Wait!" she called.

"We don't have a lot of time," he argued.

"You have to hit me or something. I can't mosey i unscathed and claim I was being held hostage. They' charge me with Frankie's murder and I'll be stuck in th same situation you've been in for the past four years. I that what you want?"

"I can't do it."

"You have to."

Clayton cursed. "I really, really can't."

Tory rolled her eyes. "I'm not really excited about th concept, but it's necessary."

"Tory?"

"Oh, good Lord! Give me your shoe."

"What?"

She held out her hand. "Your shoe?"

Clayton slipped off the loafer and gave it to her. Afte a brief, silent countdown, Tory reared back and the smashed herself square on the head.

Chapter Eighteen

"Do you need a doctor?" Seth Landry asked as he escorted her out of the jail thirty-one hours after she'd shown up and surrendered.

"No, the EMTs gave me two stitches when I got here."

She had a splitting headache. It was cold and she was tired and worried. Very worried. Shivering, she glanced around the dark streets of Jasper as if seeing it for the first time. It wasn't that the town was different. She was different.

"How about a lift home?"

She looked up at the familiar face and offered a weak smile. "Isn't that some sort of conflict of interest? The judge released me ROR on the aiding-and-abetting charges but the Las Vegas police are probably going to charge me in connection with Frankie Hilton's murder."

"My brother didn't steal your gun and shoot that guy. I don't care how many notes he writes."

Tory shifted her purse on her shoulder as they walked toward the police car parked on the side street. "I told you, Sheriff. I didn't see the shooting, and I didn't know Clayton had written that note."

In truth, she had hurt her head so badly that she forg
about the note until the police retrieved it from her ba

"Clayton would never have hit you, either."

"I've been interrogated to death," Tory complaine
"I just want to go home."

"And I want to find my brother. I don't want son
gung ho rookie opening fire in hopes of making his c
reer."

While she sympathized with Seth, she wasn't abo
to say or do anything that might put Clayton in dang
"I don't know where he is," Tory insisted, waiting to fi
ish her remarks until the small green car passed b
"Badgering me won't change that."

"But you know more than you're telling," Seth cou
tered, steely anger punctuated his tone.

"I'm telling you to take me home."

IT HAD TAKEN CLAYTON longer than anticipated to fir
Davis's address then trek the thirty miles of rugged te
rain. He was cold, hungry and tired, but knowing To
was probably sitting in a cell because of him had ke
him moving.

Using trees and shrubs for cover, he zigged ar
zagged his way from the street to the back door of D
vis's house. He tried two windows before finding or
with a lock loose enough to pick. Using his pocketknif
he slid the blade up and flipped the latch to open.

After lifting the window an inch, he froze, waitin
for an alarm or any indication that the occupant ha
been alerted of his presence.

Nothing. Good deal.

He spilled into the window, landing on the floor with minimal sound. His eyes were accustomed to the dark, so only took a few seconds for him to catalog the layout.

Testing each potential spot with slight pressure, Clayton moved with slow determination.

The kitchen was a square, galley-type room with dishes in piles along the counter. As he passed by, he saw a stack of photographs illuminated by the night-light above the stove. He immediately recognized the images. Tory's apartment building. Tory leaving the building. Tory at a service station gassing the BMW. Dread spread through him like a surging tide. Realizing that Davis had been following Tory—and was most likely the one who'd tried to strangle her—made his blood boil. The notion of causing Davis Abrams pain inspired him.

He continued with purpose. Through the family room. Down the narrow walkway. Up the stairs.

Davis was a lousy housekeeper, Clayton surmised. The house had a foul smell that grew worse as he reached the second floor.

Cleanliness, it turned out, wasn't the problem.

THOUGH SETH HAD OFFERED to see her inside, Tory desperately wanted to be alone. Her energy was zapped.

Her apartment door had been repaired since last she was home. She went inside, locked the dead bolt and crumpled into a heap of tears. She stumbled to her bedroom and flung herself across the bed, staying there for a long time—hours, in fact.

It was dawn before she hoisted herself off the bed and

went into the bathroom. She bathed, did her best to get
the blood out of her hair and then dressed in soft jeans
and an even softer sweatshirt.

Outside she could hear the sounds of people starting
their days. Benign, simple days. Work, family, shopping.

"Normal things," she muttered as she made coffee
and started to hunt for something to eat.

Her appetite was nonexistent, but then, so was the
contents of her cupboards. She had a dull headache that
could have been from her injury or from not eating.
Unhitting herself wasn't a possibility, so a trip down the
street to the corner store was in order. She was willing
to do just about anything to avoid calling her office. She
didn't want to be arrested and fired in the same twenty-
four-hour period.

After grabbing her purse, she started walking. It was
a pretty, early-fall day. Slightly crisp air, gentle breeze
through leaves that hinted at the brilliant colors to come.

But she was distracted. Clayton was out there. Alone.

Pangs of emotion squeezed at her chest whenever she
thought about him. She loved him. She should have
thought of some alternative. Some plan that would have
let her see it through to the end.

The corner market was not much more than four
long aisles. Most absolute necessities were stocked,
plus every junk food ever manufactured. Tory grabbed
a small basket and looped her arm through the narrow
metal handle.

Sugar was the mother's milk of curing depression, so
Tory loaded her basket with several treats. As she tried
to decide between buying the sealed pack of ten candy

ars versus the half-pound sack of its bite-size cousin,
small boy tugged at the back of her sweatshirt.

She smiled down at the kid, guessing he was somewhere around ten. He was cute, all big blue eyes, freck-
es and bright-red hair. "Hi," she greeted. "Are you lost?"

Shaking his head, he clutched the crumpled bill Tory
potted in his chubby fingers.

"Need help finding something?" She shopped here
ften and knew parents often dispatched their children
o pick up some forgotten or depleted item.

"Are you Vic…" He stumbled over her name.

"Victoria," she supplied, much to the obvious relief
f her new young friend. Did she know him? Was he a
eighborhood kid?

"You have to go out there," he said, pointing to the
mergency exit at the back of the store.

Her phone vibrated, so she gave the boy an apolo-
etic look as she pulled it from her purse, confirmed that
t was her office yet again and ignored it. "Why would
need to go out back?" she queried softly. "You know
ne manager doesn't allow you kids to sell things on his
roperty." The policy against school fund-raisers was
vell established at her corner market. Still that didn't
top more-enterprising children from soliciting patrons.

"I'm not selling anything. There's someone waiting
or you."

"Who?" Her first instinct was the police, but that
lidn't make sense. Law enforcement didn't send small
hildren in to flush out suspects.

"I…I can't say. I'm just 'posed to tell you Clayton
vants you."

Shoving her basket into the stunned arms of the child
she dashed toward the back of the store, heart racing
He was okay.

He was here!

She was ecstatic!

She was screwed!

Her first instinct was to run, but shock—total and ab
solute—glued her in place. The small-caliber handgun
was trained on her, held by the very last person she
could ever imagine seeing.

"P-Pam?" she choked. "But you're…"

"Dead," the attractive woman finished easily. "That
was the plan. Then Clayton escaped. He always was a
resourceful guy," she mused as she used the gun to wave
Tory in the direction of the compact car parked partially
hidden behind the garbage bin. "So where is he?"

Tory clutched her purse and inched backward toward
the door. Scanning the area, she saw no signs of life, no
one to hear her screams. Her mind blurred. Snippets of
possibilities bombarded her as she tried to think of some
way out of this.

"No, no," Pam cautioned. Her gray eyes glistened
bright, cold and as devoid of emotion as the steel barrel
of her weapon. "In the car, Tory. Take me to Clayton."

"I don't know where he is," she insisted.

Pam gave a derisive little laugh. "You two have been
inseparable since his escape." Pam moved to poke Tory
with the gun. "I've been trailing the two of you."

Tory realized that was true. She recognized the small
green compact. She'd seen that car in the parking lot of
the Dallas motel. And last night, as she was leaving the

police station. And, she thought with a growing sense of dread, it had been parked outside the warehouse when Frankie was killed.

"Get in," Pam demanded impatiently. "I can kill you right now and walk away. I'm dead, remember? The cops wouldn't even think to suspect me."

Dying definitely wasn't on the top of her list, so Tory did as instructed and climbed into the passenger seat of the car. Pam made her first small mistake then, and Tory took full advantage.

Keeping her eyes peeled on her abductor as she walked around the car, Tory managed to pull her phone out of her purse and slip in under her thigh.

Good thing, too, because Pam grabbed Tory's purse and tossed it in the back, out of reach. Then she started the engine and peeled out.

"SHERIFF'S OFFICE."

Clayton used a small rag over the receiver to muffle his voice. Hopefully it would be enough. Hopefully he could pull this off.

"This is Cody Landry, may I speak to my brother?"

"Hi, Cody, this is Becky. How are you holding up?" the receptionist asked.

Clayton's heart sank. He had no idea what—if any— relationship his brother had with Seth's secretary. His decision to pretend to be Cody had been simple. Cody hadn't been home in years, so he figured it would be easier to pass himself off as the wandering brother.

"We're all concerned," he answered.

"Seth is on the road, want me to patch you through?"

"Yes." He waited, listening to a series of tones and clicks, hoping that the secretary didn't have the inclination or the technology to listen in. It was dangerous to contact his brother. But necessary. He needed to make sure Tory was safe.

"Landry," his brother's familiar voice crackled over the line.

"Five-o-seven West Craven Heights. Now."

Clayton hung up and prayed his plan worked. While he waited for Seth, he kept rummaging through Davis's house. Thus far he'd discovered copies of several incriminating documents. But nothing to solve the mystery in the second-floor bedroom.

He ransacked everything—cabinets, drawers—even going so far as to slit the cushions on the furniture to see if anything had been hidden inside. Nothing.

Perspiration beaded on his brow and as he wiped it away he heard a car pull into the drive. Plastering himself against the wall, he peered out the window and felt relieved as Seth emerged from his cruiser alone.

His brother's hand rested on his side arm as he approached the front door. Clayton turned the lock just seconds before Seth entered.

"You made good time," Clayton remarked once his brother was safely inside.

They hugged, slapping each other's backs before separating. It was obvious by Seth's scrunched face that the odor registered.

"He's upstairs," Clayton explained.

Pushing back his Stetson, Seth breathed heavily, then asked, "What the hell have you been doing?"

"I found him this way," Clayton insisted. "I'm more pissed he's dead than he is."

"I doubt that," Seth returned dryly. "Who is he and how did you end up here?"

Clayton explained the nursing home scam, the money Pam had hidden, Frankie's murder and his travels with Tory.

"You married her?" Seth croaked.

Clayton shrugged. "It seemed like the thing to do at the time. Is she okay?"

Seth nodded. "She's tough. The Feds were all over her. The Department of Corrections sent an investigator. I pushed her, but she didn't budge."

Clayton breathed guilty relief. "Did you give her a nice cell?"

Seth shook his head. "She's out," he explained. "Posted bond late last night."

Clayton had a bad, sinking feeling in the pit of his stomach. "Someone killed Davis, so there's obviously another partner in this scam. I want you to put someone on Tory around the clock until we can figure out who it is."

"Already done," Seth replied. "A plainclothes unit has been on her since I dropped her off."

"Good," Clayton said, relieved.

"No, good for you," Seth commented, genuine emotion in his eyes. "This whole scam is amazing. Pam's murder had to be connected. Which means you'll be exonerated."

Clayton allowed himself to savor this moment. "I know there will be a few miles of red tape, but no competent judge could look at the trail of bodies and not see that I was set up."

"And hopefully we can flush out the last conspirator," Seth agreed. "Any ideas?"

"I've racked my brain and torn this place to shreds," Clayton admitted.

"I can see that. My lab guys are going to have trouble finding any useful evidence."

He glanced around the room and had to agree with his brother's assessment. "That couldn't be helped. I thought Davis was the end of the line. I got a little frustrated when I found him dead. And I'm guessing he's been dead a while."

"Too long to have killed Hilton?"

Seth nodded. "Yes. But I'm pretty sure he's the guy who attacked Tory in her apartment. I know Frankie Hilton was crazy to get his hands on the money Pam hid before she was killed. I'm guessing Frankie was about to give Davis up that night at the warehouse. But Davis was already dead by then, so who killed Frankie? Who is the missing link?"

"You and Tory might have overlooked something," Seth suggested gently. He walked over to where Clayton had piled several documents. "How, exactly, did Davis fit into the scam?"

Pulling over one of the barstools, Clayton laid out what he had found. "Davis was Pam's man inside. He signed off on her fraudulent accounting. That's how she was able to skim money from the estates without anyone being the wiser."

"But only in Montana, right?" Seth asked. "He would have been useless to her certifying the estate accounts in Texas."

"I know," Clayton agreed. "But Davis was on the board of the alumni association at Hawthorne. I found lots of correspondence about that in his desk. He knew a lot about the private lives of the older alumni. I'm guessing he identified those people to Pam. Then Pam told Frankie, Frankie hastens the deaths. Pam gets appointed to handle the estates. She robs them blind and does it all in plain sight."

Seth blew out a breath. "How the hell did your ex-wife ever come up with this?"

"Beats me, but it got her killed. It got a lot of people killed."

"We're still missing a crucial piece," Seth said. "Davis couldn't have killed Frankie. You're sure he wouldn't have killed Pam. So who did?"

Chapter Nineteen

"I'm growing very bored with this," Pam sneered. "Tell me where he is. Now."

Tory pretended to be scratching her leg when in reality, she was pressing the autodial key on her concealed cell phone. "He dumped me in the woods," Tory repeated. "I don't know where he was going. I swear."

Pam reached over and jabbed Tory in the cheek with the cold, hard barrel of the gun.

"Clayton left you high and dry? Did it hurt your feelings, pathetic little Tory?" She snickered wickedly. "Do you know how much it annoyed me to watch you, day in and day out, silently lusting after my husband?"

"I didn't—"

"Shut up," Pam yelled. "My marriage was crumbling and there you were, biding your time until you could get your claws into my husband."

"Your marital problems weren't my fault," Tory mumbled.

"Sure they were," Pam insisted. "But I made sure Clayton wasn't available to you after my sudden demise. Planning is everything. And right now I'm planning a very slow, very painful death for Clayton, and you're going to get to watch."

"CAN YOU GET A FIX on the location?" Seth thundered into the phone.

"West," the dispatcher answered.

"How the hell did the unit lose her?" Clayton shouted, pounding his fist against the cruiser's dash.

"She was in a grocery store," Seth explained for the second time. "They were watching the front, not the back."

"Great system," Clayton grumbled.

The car was racing to the coordinates as they were broadcast over the car's communication system. Clayton listened as some faceless voice called out cross streets. Terror knotted his whole body and a feeling of utter uselessness had settled in his stomach.

"I never should have left her alone."

Seth stepped on the gas, urging the car ever faster. Trees were little more than green smears as they flew down the road. The car literally went airborne a few times, tires returned to the road with a bounce that jarred his neck.

"Patching through," the dispatcher said, then distant, muffled words filled the interior of the car.

Clayton's blood ran cold at the familiar voice of his dead wife.

"…I wanted him to suffer," Pam was saying. "Like I was suffering. He was taking everything from me."

Then Tory's voice challenged, "He was not. You were stealing from helpless, defenseless people. You killed some of them."

Clayton cringed. "Don't bait her, sweetheart."

But his pleas couldn't be heard. He was forced to helplessly listen as Pam—*oh my God, she isn't dead*—spoke in cold, emotionless syllables.

"They were dying anyway," Pam scoffed. "Davis and I had a nice thing going here in Montana. Only, Davis had a gambling problem and owed Frankie Hilton money. When Davis got a little behind on his debts, he brought Frankie in. Frankie helped us expand the operations. Then Frankie got the bright idea to hasten their demise. He didn't think the money was coming in fast enough. It was simple, really. Once a target was identified by Davis, Frankie sent his guy in to do the deed. Then I handled things from there."

"So what went wrong?" Tory asked.

"Clayton decided to divorce me. I had to disclose my finances to that stupid arbitrator in order to get support. I had to hide the money. If I didn't, Clayton would have been able to walk away without giving me my due."

"And the million plus you had stashed away wasn't enough?"

"For one person, maybe," Pam replied. "But thanks to that idiot Davis, it was now a three-way split. And Davis was still placing bets. He was hounding me for more money. I tried to tell him that I needed to keep it hidden until after Clayton and I finished dividing our assets."

"It must have been terrible for you. I've always said there's nothing worse than reasonable killers who can't resolve their differences amicably—ow!"

Clayton's breath caught in his throat. "Tory, baby, please stop." He didn't want to know what had caused her to cry out in pain.

"She's keeping her talking," Seth said, apparently trying to find something positive to interject.

"I was being squeezed from all sides," Pam continued. "So, I devised a way out."

"How did you manage that?" Tory asked.

Clayton was relieved to hear her voice was strong and clear.

"Careful planning. It took two months of regularly sticking an IV in my own arm, extracting my own blood and freezing it. Then I waited for the right moment, picked a fight with Clayton, defrosted and scattered the blood and made the anonymous call to the police."

"A lot of trouble. Why not just disappear?"

Pam gave a chilling little laugh. "Because Frankie and Davis would have looked for me. This way I could keep all of the money for myself, and I got the added bonus of knowing Clayton was sitting in a cage."

"But then he escaped."

"An unfortunate complication," Pam agreed. "But it worked in my favor after all. Frankie had never given up looking for the money. You two presented me with the perfect way to get rid of him. I knew Davis had—"

Two loud beeps came over the broadcast.

"Her cell battery is dying," Seth exclaimed.

"What the hell is that?" they heard Pam yell. "A telephone! You stupid little bitch!" Then there were sounds of a struggle, then nothing.

"Do something!" Clayton bellowed.

Seth grabbed the mike and began barking orders. "I want the location of that last cell transmission. Now."

THERE WAS SCRATCHING and hitting and screaming. Tory's attention was divided between the crazed woman's gun and the fact that the car was careening off the roadway.

Using every ounce of her strength, she gripped the gun, and then used it as a club, pounding in the general direction of Pam's head. It worked once. Twice. Then the whole world started spinning.

Tory's shoulder hit the window, then the windshield. One of Pam's knees caught her in the jaw. She was tumbling freely. Smashing against the four sides of the car's interior like a doll in a washing machine until the momentum was stopped by a hard, sudden jolt.

Battered and disoriented, Tory scrambled to untangle herself. Shoving Pam's slack body away, Tory kicked at the mangled remnants of the windshield until it gave way. Ignoring the broken safety glass, she reached up and hoisted herself out of the car.

She had to shimmy around twisted metal. The car had come to rest at the bottom of a ravine, hood accordioned against the trunk of a tree. Steam and fluids hissed and spurted from the heap of tangled parts as Tory stumbled backward.

Her ears were ringing and her knees buckled, causing her to crumple against the ground. Pam was still lying in the wreckage.

Move! her brain screamed. Barely able to walk on her trembling legs, she began a hand-over-hand climb upward to where a hunk of severed guardrail glimmered in the sunlight.

Using exposed roots, even small plants, Tory grabbed anything to help her navigate the steep, rocky slope. She tasted blood but kept climbing.

The ringing sound solidified into a distinct pattern. Not ringing. Sirens. Relief brought with it tears.

She was on hands and knees when two cruisers came screeching to a halt several feet away.

Clayton jumped from the car before it came to a full stop. He needed to get to her. The sight of Tory crawling along the highway, bleeding and crying ripped out his heart. He ran.

"Sweetheart?" he whispered as he gingerly brushed her hair away from her face. He kissed her tears and held her head steady. "Be still," he cautioned, then over his shoulder, he called, "Get an ambulance!"

He didn't hear any reply, but he didn't care. His only interest was to prove to himself that she was alive and reasonably well.

"Where does it hurt?" he asked.

She offered a weak smile. "Everywhere but my eyelashes."

He saw the extent of her injuries and felt a tidal wave of guilt. Her cheek was bruised and cut. Her sweater was torn, revealing a deep, purple welt. One knee poked out of her ripped jeans, bloodied and caked with a fair amount of dirt.

"I'm so sorry this happened to you. We'll get you help," he promised, turning back to see Seth and two other officers. Three men. Three guns drawn.

It took a second for his brain to process, then he instinctively covered Tory's body as bullets began to fly.

Someone yelled "clear" or "down," as the air around him filled with the smell of gunpowder. Tentatively he lifted his head and peered down the ravine. Pam's motionless body lay in the field, hand still gripping a gun.

"It's over," he whispered, turning to Tory.

She smiled with some effort, closed her eyes and passed out cold.

Epilogue

She answered her telephone on the third ring. "Hello?"

"Hi, it's Meg from Today's Temp. I've got a job for you."

Tory let out the breath she'd been holding, annoyed when the disappointment settled in. Oh, she was glad for the day job—she needed the money. But that little part of her had clung to the outside hope that it might be Clayton. It wasn't. It hadn't been, not in two months. And it wouldn't be. Her brain knew that. Unfortunately, her heart was a little slow getting with the program.

"Great, doing what?"

"Paralegal," Meg answered, clearly pleased at matching the perfect job with her client. "It's a new firm. Open-ended, too."

"That's fine," Tory hedged. "But I really am leaving." True enough. Her apartment was almost packed. Boxes were sealed and labeled.

"Whatever. Here's the address," Meg provided the information. "He sounds dreamy, by the way."

"I'll put in a good word for you," Tory promised before she hung up.

Selecting a conservative blue suit, she dressed quickly, filled her travel mug with coffee and headed for the bus stop. Her insurance company was dragging their heels on replacing the BMW, and her bank account was in no shape for a big-ticket purchase.

It took her the better part of an hour and two transfers to reach the location. It turned out to be a small building in the early stages of renovation. From the looks of it, her temporary employer needed construction workers more than a trained legal assistant.

Shifting her bag up on her shoulder, she stepped around a bucket of plaster and went inside. Someone had stenciled the words Justice Project on the glass door.

Her heart thudded in her ears, yet she hesitated. New office. Dreamy voice. It had to be Clayton.

"Who went through the temp agency to contact me," she whispered past the lump of emotion in her throat. He could have called. She read the newspapers. He'd been exonerated and the state bar association was willing to expedite his reinstatement. He'd been given a public apology from the governor and there was even talk of a multimillion-dollar settlement for the false imprisonment.

Tory knew she could never be happy working for him. And there was the other problem. No, better to cut and run with her dignity in tact.

She spun around and nearly fell into Clayton.

He greeted her with a brilliant smile tucked behind a big bouquet of flowers. "I got hung up," he explained.

His eyes searched her face and she read uncertainty in his expression.

"I can't do this," she said frankly. "I would never have come had I known you were the employer."

"Hang on," he urged, his voice almost pleading. "Can we just talk for a few minutes?"

She hated that she was so completely unable to resist him. The day would be much easier if she could just toss her head back and march out.

"We could talk on the phone," she told him, counting the roses clutched in his hand. "Oh, that's right, I forgot. You don't know how to use a phone. Because if you did, you would have done the polite thing and called to inquire about me. You know, a simple gesture where you see if I've recovered from my near-fatal encounter with your crazed ex-wife."

"Tory?"

She barreled on. "One second out of your busy day to see how I was handling being fired from my job and being stalked for a week by photographers and reporters."

"Tory?"

"No." She wasn't stopping; she was on a roll. "Not even a quick jingle to thank me for risking my very life for you."

"Tory? Oh, forget this!"

He pulled her to him, crushing his lips to hers in a passionate, spine-melting kiss that stole her breath and dulled her brain. His tongue teased, tempted and tickled her mouth and made her groan.

And then all too soon it was over. He peered down at her with fire and excitement in his eyes. "Now can we talk?"

"You can," she teased, adjusting the hem of her jacket as she moved away from him.

He took her inside the office space, using the flowers as a pointer as he gave his tour. "This will be my office," he explained. "That's a conference room. I'm having it wired for video conferencing because I'm going to be handling cases nationwide." He stopped and grinned. "Assuming this takes off."

"I'm sure you'll be a huge hit."

"This," he continued, "will be your office."

He paused, watching her for any reaction. She purposefully kept her expression bland. "It's not as big as the other office."

He smiled. "It's still early enough to move walls around. So, what do you think?"

"What, exactly, would my job description be?"

He linked his fingers behind her waist and pulled her against him. "A lot of briefs," he promised. "Appellate work, and I'll send you back to school for a crash course on DNA."

Flattening her palms against his chest, she felt the rapid, uneven beat of his heart. "Why would I want to work for you?"

"Not *for* me," he answered his expression serious. "*With* me, Tory. We make a great team. We cracked a complicated murder-for-profit ring and got an innocent man out of prison." He kissed her forehead. "I'm the innocent man in the story, by the way."

She buried her face against his chest. "I thought you'd forgotten. Why didn't you call me?"

Using one finger, he forced her chin up, meeting her eyes. "I needed to be sure."

"Of what?"

"That I would have something to offer you."

She went very still. "Do you?"

"I think so. I hope so." He stepped back and put his hand into his pocket. "I'm using my settlement from the state to fund this place. I know you aren't that keen on Montana, but this will only be our home base. We'll review convictions and, when appropriate, work our tails off to get innocent men and women out of jail."

"That's admirable," Tory acknowledged. "I'm sure you'll do great things."

"Not without you," he insisted. "I know that now."

"I can't work with you Clayton. It would be too hard."

"Why?"

"Because."

"Why, Tory?"

She met his gaze. "Because I love you. I would wither up and die if I had to be around you every day knowing that you don't—"

"I love you."

She replayed it in her mind, making very sure she had heard him correctly. "You do?"

He nodded. "Very much. Please put this back on." He took her hand and slipped her wedding band back on her finger. "Please, Tory. We're great together. We can do something amazing. But it will only matter if I can do it with you. Please say yes. Please."

She grinned and felt as if her heart might explode from sheer happiness. "Yes. The ring stays on," she told him, then held up her hands. "But I can't work for you."

He seemed to deflate before her eyes. "Why not? You're brilliant. You're organized. I know you'll love the work. Together we can—"

"I really can't work for you. At least not full-time."

"You got another job?"

She nodded. "A very demanding job. I've already made a commitment, and it has to be my first priority, so I'd only be able to work when it doesn't conflict with my new responsibilities."

"Can you get out of it?" he asked.

"No."

"Will you at least try?"

"No."

"Why not?"

"Because I can't."

"Of course you can. What kind of job can't you get out of?"

"Motherhood."

She got secret pleasure out of seeing his shocked expression.

Clayton grabbed her and gave her a soft, tender kiss. "Were you planning on telling me?"

"You'll never know, will you?" she teased.

"Any more surprises?"

She simply smiled, then said, "Let's hope so."

* * * * *

Don't miss the next book in
THE LANDRY BROTHERS *series,*
FILM AT ELEVEN,
available in July from Intrigue.

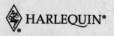

HARLEQUIN®

INTRIGUE

Return to

M^CCALLS' MONTANA

this spring
with

B.J. DANIELS

Their land stretched for miles across
the Big Sky state...all of it hard-earned—
none of it negotiable. Could family ties
withstand the weight of lasting legacy?

AMBUSHED!
May

HIGH-CALIBER COWBOY
June

SHOTGUN SURRENDER
July

Available wherever Harlequin Books are sold.

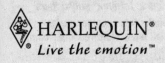

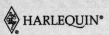

IT'S A JUNGLE OUT THERE...
AND WE'RE TURNING UP THE HEAT!

ONE WOMAN.
ONE DEADLY VIRUS.
ONE SCANDALOUS COVER-UP.

Get ready for an explosive situation as Dr. Jane Miller races to stop a dangerous outbreak and decide which man to trust.

THE AMAZON STRAIN
by Katherine Garbera

May 2005

Available at your favorite local retailer.

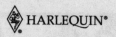